WHAT... IS...
HAPPENING?

GERALD AGNEW

ISBN
978-1-957378-92-3 (Paperback)
978-1-957378-91-6 (eBook)
978-1-958122-18-1 (Hardcover)

DEDICATION

Behind every author (hopefully a successful one here!) lies his friends, family; people who care and who have egged him on with his venture. I have been blessed with three such people and I wish you to be aware whom you can credit (or curse!) for the putting together of the effort which follows. Why is it that when you need people like this around you they appear as if by magic?!

I wish to thank, with all my heart, my long suffering wife who finally got me off my intellectual duff and told me "Write the book, dammit". I was married to her for forty-two years (cancer took this brilliant woman), and she STILL had to talk like this to get me going! There is no question that without her this would not have been written.

My thanks to my granddaughter, Shylee, who continually encouraged me to put the ideas I had been talking to her about into some sort of format which made sense. She "got me organised" and put the ideas into a meaningful pattern from the chaos they were in before. Wise beyond her twenty-eight years, she gave me the sense of "You have good information. Get it out to as many people as possible". Thank you, Shylee!

Finally, to a wise woman named Lisa Boag-Guidi who is a veritable font of ideas, I give my sincere thanks. When I was talking to her about the book and wondering how I should get the relevant ideas together she merely said "Why don't you divide the book into several segments, and then expand each one"? Such a simple idea and one that I am sure would never have occurred to me if I was left to my own devices. The best ideas are the simplest! Thank you, Lisa!

TABLE OF CONTENTS

INTRODUCTION

WHY ARE YOU SO CAUGHT (AS IN A TRAP) IN TODAY'S FINANCIAL WORLD?

I have been considering writing a book ever since my granddaughter suggested it. At that time I was busy, in my retirement, writing a newsletter devoted to global financial and cultural matters. My granddaughter can be very persuasive however!

In my many years in the financial markets, culminating as a Senior Foreign Exchange Advisor with Bank of America in Seattle, Washington (I am a Canadian citizen) I came to the conclusion that what we are seeing and hearing about our globalized economy could be assessed via a thorough study of economics and what makes it work. This is a study of how a particular culture influences what we see and consider about such trends. My granddaughter, and then my family, suggested that I could reach many more people than I could with a simple newsletter.

I agreed with this and so was born "What ... IS... Happening?". In my book I wish to try and tell people, based on my forty years plus of financial experience, why they are feeling so "caught" by what they read every day in their favorite medium, whatever that may be. It seems that whatever our leaders, politicians and financial specialists tell us, nothing ever seems to get better.

We suffer from squeezed incomes and whatever we try to do to enjoy what our societies offer us, we can never fully savor the fruits of our labors. Debt mounts up as we borrow to bridge the differences between our wants and our incomes and throughout all of this we constantly read about the CEO of a major corporation enjoying yet another multi-million dollar bonus. This lucky person enjoys such riches for apparently doing little more than firing thousands of local workers and sending the jobs to China, Cambodia, Bangladesh or someplace that many of us have never heard of.

New records are set with the number of freshly minted billionaires increasing every year, while we slog along wondering how the dentist bills are going to be paid.

Resting up after a crippling leg injury suffered last September, I chanced to reacquaint myself with the analysis of a noted financial author who has been in the business for decades: Marty Armstrong. The man is a genius in my view and he has discovered that markets operate according to various cycles.

No, nothing new there, but he showed again and again that a multiple of Pi (ie the 3.1416 number we learned about in high school to discover the area of a circle given its radius) dominates many of the financial markets we see. His hypothesis was a simple one. We should forget the hyperbole surrounding what the financial press says about financial panics, as the various reporting media tend to be swept up in the emotions of the moment. All of what we see can be defined on longer term considerations, he says, and that is what we should be looking at.

Fascinated, and being bedridden with little to occupy my time, I started to wonder if our culture itself could be subject to the same Pi Cycle. Remarkably, I think that it CAN! I started with a very old template (The Remarkably, I think that it CAN! I started with a very old template (The Bible) for the principles which America was supposed be founded on: a Christian nation which is subject to cycles, and this we have apparently been warned about for thousands of years.

No, please do not roll your eyeballs at this mention of The Bible (which another of my daughters did when I told her about this project). Hear me out. You have not wasted your money in buying this book – really and truly!

Without some sort of mathematical proof of what I am writing about, I might agree with you and indulge in eyeball rolling myself! But there IS proof and thanks to the idea I obtained from Mr. Armstrong I decided to go ahead with all that I am about to show you. I would like to give you one small example of what lies ahead in Chapter One.

I simply cannot believe that all of what follows is a mathematical coincidence to be frank. Look up the Old Testament; in particular the Book of Daniel 8:14 where the two angels are talking about 2300 "mornings and evenings". I started to play with Pi on my hand-held calculator and found the following – with Pi valued here at 3.14159 (my calculator won't go any higher than five decimal places!). 2300/3.14159/3.14159 = 233.039. Now 233 is a Fibonacci Number (part of a sequence formed by adding the two previous whole numbers in a sequence together, starting at 1 – ie 1,2,3,5,8,13,21,34,89,144,233 etc.) and I also found out that 233 ties in beautifully with the story of the United States and its founding in 1776. Want to see more? Go to Segment One – The Bible and Pi, and what it says about the next few years.

Fibonacci analyses, by the way, are very useful for equity (stock market) traders in assessing various heights and depths of markets, and after a rise (or fall) just how far a rebound can come. In other words, they are not an idle curiosity factor but something with real usefulness for a major trader.

They also have a very good practical benefit in assessing the future of the USA (and the Western world, as it is all tied together via the large-scale use of the US$, the world's Reserve Currency). Anyhow, have a look at what I have found as it does tie in with the thesis of this book in my opinion.

Let us continue with the 2300 analysis. We take 2300/233.039 and arrive at 9.86596. Divide this by 3.14159 and we get (drum roll) ... 3.14159; in other words, Pi almost exactly! So, this caught my attention, and with plenty of time to analyses other possible Biblical

Pi cycles I certainly had the opportunity to do such an exercise! There is a GREAT deal more interestingly enough, and I shall be putting this in Chapter One for your perusal.

There are many other ideas which I wish to share with you and we can do this in the remaining chapters of this book. There are sections on "Oil and Politics" which would also include a good look at the giant Tar Sands in Alberta, Canada (my home province) and how it can affect what you pay for your weekly (more frequent?) fill-up at the pump.

It also says a lot about how the Western World operates, given that so much revolves around the price of this critical commodity. What about US politics and what can we say about the possibility of a President Hillary Clinton?

Ah, there is so much to help you understand "What ... IS ... happening"?

SEGMENT ONE

CHAPTER ONE

◆◆◆◆◆◆

THE GENIUS OF MARTY ARMSTRONG
AND SOME BIBLICAL PI (NO, NOT PIE!)

I have mentioned the redoubtable Marty Armstrong already in the introduction to this book, but it occurs to me that many of you have no idea who the man is. I had better explain, hadn't I?

He is an analyst, par excellence, and was responsible (although he probably doesn't know it in the least!) for me finding the extraordinary examples of how Pi and Fibonacci analysis are seen in the Books of Daniel and Revelation in The Bible. He also has found the economic properties of the number 4.3 (more commonly expressed as twice this as a cycle based of 8.6 times a unit of time – generally a year).

He found this, apparently, by looking at the time which it takes for the Earth, as measured by the long term movement of the North Pole, to make a full circle/trip around the sky at night. This takes 25,800 years and is an exact multiple of 8.6 – 3,000 times. Now I have no idea why his discovery is so and why such a huge number of years has an effect on much smaller cycles such as what he analyses for his readers, but it does. As such I would be foolish not to take note of what he says and has proved. Accordingly I do read what he has to say.

I do not use this number to assess my Biblical Pi Cycles, but it is with great interest I see that what I come up with and what he derives are close to exact in assessing the future. My Biblical cycles and his Pi and 8.6 ("Polar Cycle" to give it a name) show that we must pay close attention to his discovery and how he has determined it has such an effect in the real world.

I have never seen him refer to The Bible for his work, but of interest is a small comment from the Book of Daniel (12:11) which speaks of a time when the "regular burnt offering is taken away" and when the abomination that desolates is set up is 1290 days. The next verse speaks of those people being happy who will persevere until the 1335th day. Now this tells us that what Armstrong has found has Biblical significance as 1290 is exactly divisible by 8.6; some 150 times.

No, I do not know (yet!) what the 150 stands for. I also note that 1335 is almost an exact Pi multiple. So, we ask about this. Why did the angel advising Daniel tell him about 1290 days? Why did he inform him about 1335 days? Why did the angel use these apparently strange numbers (as opposed to something like 1300 and 1350: something "nice and round")?

There is clearly something significant relating to these "strange numbers", and the answer must clearly be that they are both to be seen in a cycle and that, possibly without knowing about it, Armstrong has stumbled into a set of cycles which are, in effect, ratified by The Bible. Is this why they are so accurate and why he is so highly sought after to advise nations (China – PRC apparently thinks very highly of him it seems)?

I shall also make references, as the reader will see as s/he (she/ he contraction; do you like it?) progresses throughout the various Segments and Chapters, to Armstrong's major work: the War Cycle. This horrible thing he has worked on for a long time and apparently it goes back, in one form or another, for centuries.

It shows, for a reason which I do not fully understand, that mankind engages in war – either directly or indirectly – every quarter century. I do not mean a life/death struggle for the very fate of the human race, but rather we see one of three things: a major conflict, a medium sized one (a la Korea), or else a major change of a dominant philosophy somewhere in the world which has a major global impact.

Let me give you an example of this, just dating back to the early twentieth century. In 1914, and we see the centenary of this in 2014, was the First World War (aka The Great War as it is known in Britain) which started in August of that year ("The Guns of August" is a major work describing this terrible conflict). In 1939, just after the end of August, we saw the German invasion of Poland which started the Second World War. That is to say twenty-five years on from 1914.

In August 1964 we saw a major decision by the powers-that-be in the United States (then at the very zenith of its global authority: politically; culturally; and economically) to start the ball in motion for the desperately expensive and divisive war in Southeast Asia: Viet Nam.

At that time, the Pentagon carried out what we might describe today as a False Flag operation in the Gulf of Tonkin which led to the first US incursions into that country early in 1965 (after the Presidential election in November 1964, the cynic might add). In 1989 there was no war, but the collapse of Communism under the last significant Soviet leader Mikhail Gorbachev, would certainly qualify as a major change in how the world is run in my book!

As an aside here, I should note that there are many people (me among them as I have written about in my newsletter sometime previously) who feel that the collapse of Communism was some sort of "staged event" and that some years down the road we shall see it, or a close cousin, re-emerge.

Now we come to 2014 which is, as noted, the centenary of World War One. It is a War Cycle year and while we came close to something happening in Syria and the Middle East in 2013, the cycles were not correct then, and we have moved to 2014 where the ongoing ruckus in The Ukraine (as this is being written in Spring 2014) is threatening to explode into all sorts of nasty things.

We should look, under this War Cycle, for something to happen in the last six months of this year as Armstrong has pointed out that this time of the year is not a period which is friendly to peace. Yep! Have to agree with this one! Japan is also, for the first time since its shattering defeat in World War Two, starting to flex its muscles in its area of the Pacific and one wonders if there will be a clash between Japan and China (PRC) before all of this is over. There might also be a clash in Korea again.

What defined Korea was its liberation from Japanese colonial oppression in 1945. So, 2014-1945 = 69 years which almost exactly 22 times Pi. Twenty-two is something which I find very interesting as well, as we shall see just a little later on in the current First Segment of my book. I am left wondering if a 69 year gap in conflicts is also something which we should carefully access as we move forward. Just for fun, 69/22 is also almost equal to Pi (22*3.1416 = 69.115). Powerful stuff here! PLEASE NOTE THAT AS THE BOOK GOES ON, I REFER TO "PI NUMBERS". A PI NUMBER IS ONE WHICH IS ALMOST EXACTLY DIVISIBLE BY PI AND THIS MEANS A GREAT DEAL IN MY SYSTEM OF BIBLICAL PI ANALYSIS!

I shall probably be referring to Armstrong's work as I look at various economic cycles as they play out in the United States. PLEASE remember that because of the primacy of the US$ across the world, it remains the world's reserve currency – a place where governments store their reserve cash. What transpires in New York City and Washington is of critical importance as we move towards whatever awaits us.

In particular, I am looking at Armstrong's date of October 1, 2015 where he writes that his study of cycles tells him that we are looking at an event which will cause the world's sovereign bond markets (where global governments go to borrow the funds they need for day-to-day operations) to start to implode. Now, how many times have we read about how the US is in serious straits because it borrows so much? What do you think will happen if it becomes difficult for the US Treasury to raise the funds it requires?

It will not be good and Armstrong feels that while this unfortunate cycle starts to becomes deeper and more painful, it will probably spill over to the rest of the world. By the way, in looking at Armstrong's Oct. 1, 2015 date I looked at my Biblical Pi cycles and found that all of this nastiness starts in October 14, 2015. This is clearly very close to Armstrong's date (and I shall detail all of what I have found in this Segment of the book) and we must pay close attention in how he and I look at all of this.

Armstrong has been in this business for a long time and in years gone by (in the 1980s) he was so good at what he did that he could demand, and receive, sums to make him the highest paid economist in the United States (Wikipedia).

He was arrested and jailed for seven years for contempt and the rumour mill is that he would not give to US authorities his techniques for his exceptionally accurate forecasting analysis. Rightly or wrongly, he is now out of custody and is forecasting yet again. It is these most recent calls which we shall be interested in for the first segment of this book.

He is, perhaps understandably, bitter towards the economic and political future of the United States. I leave what he has to say to my readers to assess for themselves. All I can do is to deeply analyse what I believe lies ahead using my own analysis, which is what this book is all about.

All right, I have written fairly extensively on Mr. Armstrong. However, this is my book and you may be asking – justifiably in my view – where do I get all of the information I am going to present to you in the coming Chapters and Segments?

In the main, I have simply referred to the newsletters which I send out to my readers three times a week. For these, when I was writing them, I did a fair piece of research and so I believe that they are accurate as to the date they were written. In any event, the purpose of this book is the same as when I wrote my newsletters: to try and make a reader think and consider what might lie ahead and, therefore, try to see that there may be other possibilities to consider going forward.

There are always two sides to every story and while it is so nice and easy to simply pick up the daily newspaper (on-line or otherwise) and browse the editorial to see what the "correct" thinking is, I would like readers to consider other possibilities. They may amaze you!

In any event, I wish to write several "Segments" to make up this book. They will comprise the look at the Biblical analysis I have been referring to. Within this first segment there will be various chapters looking at the math of Pi and Fibonacci analysis. Why is this? I firmly believe that to write a book on this subject must present more than just "Daniel means this or that" or "Revelation really means something very different because ... just because".

If I fail to deliver on the mathematical analysis to the reader's satisfaction, well so be it. I am still going to try, and other chapters in this first segment will carry on this belief of mine. Other segments will be divided into similar breakdowns (called chapters) and they will deal with, oil (THE biggie as we move forward, of that I am convinced) and the attempts to procure ever more of this critical commodity by the powers-that-be in Washington. And that is probably quite enough for Segment One, Chapter One!

SEGMENT ONE

CHAPTER TWO

$\bullet\,\blacklozenge\,\blacklozenge\,\blacklozenge\,\blacklozenge\,\bullet$

LET'S HAVE SOME FIBONACCI PI!

No, no – not that kind of "pie"! I am not talking about some unusual fruit confection, but rather the mathematical variety which I have been alluding to. This is the number 3.1416 (although it is a mathematical expression which goes on forever) and which, if we multiply it by the diameter of a circle, we find to a very close approximation its circumference. Isn't the idea of a circle somehow appropriate given that we are looking at financial and cultural cycles?

If indeed this IS appropriate, then why shouldn't (as I have been hinting at so far) we use Pi to further tell our tale of a series of terrible occurrences soon to hit the United States and the world as well through the mechanism of the US$ being the global reserve currency? We can and now we shall.

To establish the validity of Pi (which I stumbled across while convalescing last October), I looked at the 2300 "mornings and evenings" in Daniel. Recently, I looked at this again and found another Pi linkage. Let revisit the number 2300 and wonder how many years it actually is. The key thing here is how people "way back when" measured a year.

The best I could come up with was 366 days which was used in Rome when various climatologists (and I use the term very loosely when measured against what people today can do with similar sets of data) had to use to work out the length of a year. Yes, I know that this 366 day number will not work over long periods of time as distortions will build and these will impact planting seasons and so forth.

Nevertheless, I used this as it is probably the time frame of reference which the angels in Daniel would have seen that mankind knew about when making their Divine call for the 2300 mornings and evenings. It turns out that 2300/366 = 6.2842 and that twice Pi equals 6.2832 which is extremely close indeed; a difference of just 0.016% – hardly worth mentioning!

It made me wonder again about whether two times Pi can be found in other bits and pieces of End Times analysis, and (you guessed it!) it CAN! Even more interesting is that it directly relates to time lines which are found in Armstrong's financial crisis date (Hey! don't forget my contribution here!). It is my contention that the End Times, lying directly ahead, relate to a major financial disturbance (there is very definitely a "Disturbance in the Force" here!).

We are not looking at a coincidence. The writers of The Bible have placed before us, if we can find these things (and I am sure that I have barely scratched the surface with my rather fortunate discoveries to date), a very interesting commentary on our future history which was written millennia ago, but has not yet played out in real time. There is one other bit of seeming trivia here in Daniel. One of the angels addressing Daniel said that the contents of what Daniel was told were to remained "sealed up until the time of the end". If my book is helping to unseal them, and I give sincere thanks to Higher Beings, then surely it is yet another indication that our immediate future is what Daniel was shown.

Now let me make a few references to my newsletter on this subject. Immediately, I wish to start assessing what this financial crisis could be and what are the relevant dates which accompany such a disaster. Let us simply say that for now it is fairly easy to see that the cause for our troubles must be the monster called "debt".

Yes I know that the average American has borrowed him/herself into oblivion over the past few decades, and all of this was probably done to maintain a standard of living which these people apparently felt they were, in some sense, owed. I cannot debate the validity of such a belief, I can merely note it with regret. This grave concern must stem from the huge debts being run up with the monster interest rates which can only act as a severe drag on the economy.

That is, of course, only one element of the US debt burden. We must also consider the accumulated debts of municipal and State spending in the US (which is considerable) and then we come to Washington's contribution to all of this insanity. Is this the right word?

Unfortunately, it is. With the US Congress showing all of the backbone of a wet noodle, we are ballooning the debt levels to $ 17.5 trillion as of April 24, 2014. It is this we hear about all the time with the GOP in Congress declaiming the Democratic White House and, unfortunately, the reverse is also true as Administrations from both parties seem to outdo themselves in wild and irresponsible spending. It is not getting any better, sorry to say, and will probably get worse especially if the economy continues to waffle endlessly in the aftermath of the 2007/08 mortgage debacle.

I rant and rave about all of this, but it seems that if this monster debt burden comes adrift it would be the cause of the disaster which I think Daniel and Revelation are both looking at. The latter Biblical Book suggests that debt and its corrupting influence will be a killer for the economy and society in general. We shall examine this a bit later on.

It is what Armstrong has been looking at, as have I. I am scared to death to be honest, but if all of this was seen with an angel talking to St. John on the Island of Patmos in about the year 94 AD, then the momentum building towards a dissolution of this debt (and its knock-on equivalents across the globe do not forget) must be incredible and completely unstoppable.

Let's finish off this Chapter with some more Pi/Fibonacci analysis for you. Oh dear! I wish, with all of the sorrow which I am writing about WAS a nice piece of Fibonacci Pie! I have no idea what that would taste like, but surely it has to be better than the bitter taste now in my mouth!

I think the best way to proceed would be explaining what 233 is and how it relates to the US specifically. Well, it is a major Fibonacci number which is used in financial (equity/stock market) analysis as we have seen earlier on. It directly relates to the US and we saw this in my cursory analysis about Daniel in the Introduction. Now let us look at the founding of the United States which traditionally dates from the signing and publicizing of the Declaration of Independence on July 4, 1776.

If we take this date and move forward 233 years, we come to 2009. Return to the comments of the "Twice Pi" argument above which related to the 2300 morning and evenings. This prophecy equates to twice Pi when converted to years on a 366-day basis. In terms of years (again!) this is six years 102 days. Adding this onto July 4, 2009 we come to October 14/15, 2015 which is just about what Armstrong's date of October 1, 2015 is! This quite beyond the realm of coincidence in my mind. Let us explore this a bit further to finish off this chapter.

Fibonacci analysis is very good for analytical work in stocks/equities as we have discussed. However, how accurate is this in reality for the average person to read these lines and nod their head in some sort of agreement? The rule of thumb is that we have a precise Fibonacci target year, in this case 1776 + 233 or 2009, but that rounding and the like can occur and mess things up, but only a little bit.

Therefore, I can say that for the purposes of this work ALL analysis must fall within a +,- 1 year band. This means that for this Fibonacci analysis to be valid it cannot occur before 2008 or after 2010 which is still a fairly narrow band. If one wishes to look at 2008, we see the real start to the mortgage debacle (the so-called "sub-prime" lending crisis) which made financial headlines across the world.

In 2010 we saw the bottom of a secondary bear market that this banker foolishness started (The primary bottom was, of course, in the Fibonacci Year 2009). So we have good dates to look at the current financial difficulties in the world (for we are still seeing bad balance sheets from the 2008 collapse; the proof of this is the huge amount of Fed money being poured into the financial system month after month). Therefore 2009 is not out of the question as an accurate US end date for the 233 Fibonacci number analysis.

With this being correct, the Oct. 14/15, 2015 date is also reasonable. This is, of course, unless Armstrong and myself are both out-to-lunch on all of this and the theory of Pi cycles is wrong. To be honest I do not agree to my missing of lunch in the least. Pi is correct!

Let's push on to more (and meatier!) Pi and Fibonacci analysis in Chapter Three of this first segment. I wish to talk with you about political instability in the US and some dates which you may wish to mark down. I am not happy with what lies ahead and we shall now see what sorts of Pi analysis can be used to tell you what is probably going to be what.

SEGMENT ONE

CHAPTER THREE

✦✦✦✦✦

LET'S HAVE SOME MORE FIBONACCI PI! (APPETITE STILL THERE?!)

And if you thought that all of what I had to offer you on Biblical analysis (particularly as it has to do with market crashes and the like), was written in Chapter two, one might also think that what moves the stock markets overall and (by extension) the US economy, is something which is completely random. By definition therefore, it cannot be known by neither traders or regular citizens. You would be wrong!

There is an old saying that "There is a Divinity that shapes our ends" and I can think of nothing better to demonstrate this than by a long term analysis of what the stock market has done since 1953. Yes, as you may have guessed by now, this date is one which is direct derived from America's founding date of 1776 and is directly related to a simple derivative of, what else, Pi!

Let me now quote from my newsletter – two of them actually – in which I looked at all of this in some depth. It is amazing what is to be found from the simple number 3.1416. I wonder how much else lies out there for the enterprising reader to find for him/herself?! (Go for it!).

Note that the mathematical symbols used seem to be fairly standard. However, let me simply say that Pi^0.5 is the square root of Pi, Pi^0.3333 is the cube root, and Pi^0.25 is the fourth root. This means that a square root is a number which when multiplied by itself comes to Pi. It means that a cube root is a number which when multiplied by itself three times come to Pi, and so on. Let's see what I wrote:-

"Late last year I wrote, for the newsletter, a series of articles on the number Pi (ie 3.1416) and how it related to the Book of Daniel in the Old Testament and to the Book of Revelation in the New. I looked at various interesting possibilities (all based off a chance bit of analysis I performed on Daniel's 2300 "mornings and evenings", which is to be found in Daniel 8:14).

"There were some curious yet fundamental Fibonacci numbers (233 in the main, which seem to be intimately tied together with the current history of the United States) which when added to dates from America's early founding - principally 1776 – gave some very notable results.

"These essays from last year can now be referred to as 'ancient history' but again, quite by chance, I found some more unexpected things which tell of US history in the early twentieth century, and early twenty-first. Perhaps there is indeed a Divinity which shapes our ends!?

"When I wrote about these Pi Cycles initially, I thought there was something else but didn't know what it was. Now I do! (I think so anyway!). I was watching the first of the movie series 'Twilight' a few weeks ago when the 'hero' of the movie talked briefly about 1.7725 which the leading lady then identified as the square root of Pi. Idly, I then started to play with my calculator (!), and looked at the square, cube, and fourth roots of Pi. The following is what I found.

"Pi = 3.1416 "Pi^0.5 = 1.7725 "Pi^0.3333 = 1.466 (reasonable as my calculator does not have cube root buttons) "Pi^0.25 = 1.331 "I also saw (and this provided me with the idea to move along in this vein) that some Fibonacci numbers are directly related to Pi in multiples. "For example 987 is a Fibonacci number, and 100*(Pi^2) almost exactly equals this! (Get out your calculator and have a look!). Additionally, in using Fibonacci analysis we can use this sort of thing for cycles. For example, we can use the first significant digits in such analysis, so the above Pi functions can be used as 177; 146; and 133. "This what we often see in such analysis. Co-incidentally (?) we see that the number above in the 987 analysis and Pi^2 (ie 100) is used to move the decimal two places to the right in the Pi roots above (ie 177, 146, and 133). It makes them nearly equal in current history other words. Is this important? Very definitely it is! Please keep reading tomorrow!".

Then, the next day, I wrote as follows:-

"In my original Pi Cycle analysis, I looked at 1776 and added 233 and so forth. This is all correct, but now we see that there are other possibilities. "1776 + 133 (fourth root from above) = 1909. It is clear that the roots of Pi (ie square, cube, and fourth roots as above) and the date 1776 are all interlinked. Therefore, the founding of the United States is of critical importance to the world going forward and has always been so as it gathered its strength in moving towards the seminal period now upon us (as I mentioned in the Pi Cycle analysis from last year). Let's look at some numbers now.

"1909+ standard Fibonacci numbers, in a series, now looks like this- "1909+ 5 = 1914. World War One which really started to change the face of the Earth. "1909+ 8 = 1917. US commits itself to this great change in the world by joining the Great War. Russian Revolution/ Communism takes over. "1909+13 = 1922. I am not sure what this date represents, even after all sorts of research - BUT 1776 + 146 (Cube root of Pi) = 1922. We can then say, once again, that Pi numbers are inextricably linked to the immediate future history (if this is not a paradox!) of the United States. I can go one step further. "The United States is SO important to the world (principally through the mechanism of the dollar as the world's Reserve Currency) that what happens to this nation is going to have major impacts on the rest of the planet. I think this is the message of The Revelation as shown to St. John on Patmos.

"How can I continue to apparently obsess over this financial angle? Well, have a look at the amazing Fibonacci numbers a couple of paragraphs further below (scaled off the year 1953) – ALL of which are related by the founding of the United States in 1776. "To finish the current table, we see - "1909+21 = 1930. Great Depression and major secondary stock market crash – THE Crash in many respects. "1909+34 = 1943. Year (plus one) of first controlled nuclear reaction in Chicago (and consequent development of the Atomic Bomb). "1909+55 = 1964. Height of US empire financially, economically, and militarily, and the Gulf of Tonkin crisis (also a War Cycle Year) which started the US on its current monetary difficulties. "Oh, yes! Let's play with your mind a little bit here. We are currently observing the centenary of the end of World War One. This was 100 years ago, and falls nicely on Armstrong's War Cycle (see 1914 above). It is clear, well to my numbers obsessed mind, that the year 2014 – this year – could well be monumental. Now let us assess the financial problems related to 1776 and another root value of Pi (the fourth root in this case) to finish off this essay tomorrow".

The next day I finished off this new Pi cycle material as follows:-

"Consider 177-133 (one level of Pi subtracted from another) and we get 44. Now 1909 (from yesterday) + 44 = 1953 which I have been told, by someone who has studied this for many years (now sadly deceased), that the major prophecies in the Great Pyramid came to an end in ... the year 1953! I also note that this is related to the founding of the United States and is the sum of 1776 + 177 (!). "More than coincidence? This person also told me that the prophecies in the Great Pyramid mentioned the crash of the stock market in 1929/30. What he DIDN'T tell me was that the rest of the major market crashes in US market history are ALL related to this number. The following table now tells me that what lies ahead for the United States and the world are financial in nature. The numbers/dates are all tops or crashes, which does not look good going forward at all!

"Have a look (as noted from above) - "1953+ 5 = 1958 or a major recession year in the US "1953+ 8 = 1961 Now nothing happened this year, but 1962 (ie Fibonacci + one {which is allowable, see earlier on in this segment}) was a very bad year "1953+13 = 1966 or the top of the US stock market for decades to come in real terms. A major top in other words! "1953+21 = 1974. Major market decline in an over-bought market amidst the oil related effects from the Gulf War. "1953+34 = 1987. Major market crash, probably related to programme trading. (Remember that one?!). "1953+55 = 2008. Major market crash and near collapse of the global financial system because of the sub-prime mortgage mess. "How's them apples?! (What happens in 2042 I wonder, which is 1953+89?). The market tops have progressed in increasing levels of seriousness. In 1958 we saw a deep recession but not catastrophically serious. In 1966 we saw a substantial long term top, and in 1974 the top and subsequent decline were even more so.

"In 1987 this was still deeper, as the new derivatives and programme trading nearly shattered everything. It may have been, in retrospect, some sort of warning about leveraging the banking/financial systems as was then being done. As usual, when impossibly large sums of money are being played with via trading games, this warning (as soon as the immediate dangers had passed) was completely ignored. "The entire financial industry nearly collapsed in 2008 with the sub-prime fiasco (and may yet do so as the knock-on effects are still being felt). Therefore, if we make it to 2042, the system probably does collapse and it will collapse so badly that there will probably not be any real hope of restoring this Wall Street money machine to its former glory ever again. It will probably be that serious, if anybody wishes to place bets that far in advance!

"Finally, I do not know if I was 'guided' in some manner to discover all of these things both in this series of essays and from last year. I am not doing this for self-glorification but with a sense of strong humility. If I have been shown the way, then I give thanks to Him who took the time to point all of these things out to me. "My sense now tells me that I am unlikely to find any more interesting bits of future history related to Pi and Fibonacci. Therefore, to my readers, just have a look at all of this from now and last year and just think and ponder what it could all mean. I believe the math is not to be refuted, so what DO all of these cycles have to say? Is it all so gloomy?". End of the newsletter quotes.

So, is it indeed "all so gloomy"? I am so very sorry to tell you that it is indeed this; and probably much more. How can this be? Well, the underlying idea of this book is that we are living in The End Times. What is this period, and why is it so significant? The Books of The Bible have spoken of this many, many times. In essence, mankind is to experience something REALLY dreadful which will repay us for all of the wickedness which has been committed throughout our history.

We can say that it is a time when, literally, "The sins of the father will be visited upon the son". Some have spoken of this as a washing of the immense karmic debts under which we are all labouring. These are individual debts but also national debts which have covered the whole world in iniquity.

The retribution will be so severe that as Christ himself told His disciples on the Mount of Olives just before He was arrested, that no flesh would be saved. The following total destruction would be so intense that if it were not for The Elect there would be nothing left at all. We are in that much trouble!

So, with this in mind and the fact the The Lord has said (millennia ago, so it is all planned out) mankind has to suffer in general, our period of history today seems to be the first real chance to exact Holy retribution. Our world is linked, hand and foot, to the power of the US economy and the US$ which is, to emphasise, the Reserve Currency of the world. Therefore if there is to be a "payback" for all that has been done which is wrong, it seems plausible that this will be accomplished in our generation and probably will start in the very near future.

This is what Fibonacci and Pi have to say about all of this and being a money professional I am inclined to agree. In any event, as you have seen from what has been written already, we have the War Cycle this year to start things off with the proverbial "bang" (sorry about that!) and then at the end of next year the financial unraveling will hit hard.

After this, with confidence in the scores of trillions of dollars in global debt badly damaged, I do not see any realistic way of stopping this freight train. As confidence is a difficult, if not impossible, item to regain once lost, things will slide from bad to worse very quickly indeed. The End Times scenario is quite valid in my sorry view.

Now what happens next? Can we measure this by our Fibonacci/Pi methods. Yes, regrettably we can. Now I must talk to you about some more measurements which come from the Book of Revelation and which also tie in with what I have been writing.

Let us look at the Seventh Seal where it states that "There was silence in Heaven for the space of about half an hour". Given that we are looking at the best part of two thousand years between today and when St. John was informed of what must have been nearly unintelligible things (to him anyhow), why would a major item such as the Seventh Seal deal with a tiny amount of time like half an hour?

What I believe is that one day in Heaven is one thousand years "down here", as is written elsewhere in The Bible. If we extrapolate the half hour from this ratio, we get that half an hour there is equal to about 20.8 years down here.

I note that the time quoted is "about half an hour", so if we extend the 20.8 years to 22 years, we are now at about 31/32 minutes which is certainly fitting the "about" time measurement (in Heaven time of course!). We can also note that this time "down here" of 22 years fits in very nicely with events which the Fibonacci/Pi time lines are suggesting. Let's see how shall we? (Please recall my comments about the number 69 earlier on and how 69 and Pi and 22 all seem to be fairly closely interlinked). The 22 year time is a Pi number (virtually exactly). That fits. I was also wondering about the "times, time, and half a time" (3.5 years) and how that ties in with things. Well, 22 is 7 times 3.1416 and I note that seven seems to crop up a lot in the Bible. Therefore, making the simple arithmetic adjustment we see that 3.5 times Pi is 11, again virtually exactly. Keep these numbers in mind please.

My greatest fear after a bond market upheaval is that there will be political instability in Washington. If one can remember the problems we had during the Debt Ceiling crisis in October/November last year, it is not beyond the realm of possibility that this may occur again; with even more force and uncertainty.

In looking at various Fibonacci/Pi possibilities (and these include the numbers I have just mentioned immediately above – the "half an hour numbers") we see that we start, as usual, with America's founding year – 1776. We add 233 to this to bring us to 2009. Onto this we can now add 11 years which seems reasonable as the 3.5 is mentioned quite often in Revelation. This brings us to the year 2020.

We can also arrive at this year by taking the War Cycle years of 2014 (itself a Pi number) and adding twice Pi to this (remember the two times Pi from Daniel which I wondered if we would see anywhere else: we do!) we come to 2020 as well. (The year of COVID!)

Finally, Armstrong in some of his amazing charts sees that 2020 is also a target year, but this is derived from his economic cycles. So, we can say US political instability arises from an economic base, which makes very good sense given where we are today and where we might very well be after the bond market debacle next year (Oct. 15, 2015).

As an interesting aside here, Armstrong mentions the year 2020 but refines it to 2020.05. So, if we now take 643 times Pi we also get 2020.05 exactly!! (Hmmm ...!). Something is very definitely brewing at about this time, but what?

Let us look at the highly respected and venerated document: The US Constitution. It is an amazing piece of work and laid the foundation for the rise to global preeminence of a group of squabbling colonists in about two centuries. This is incredible but what is its future? I read that a majority of US States have ratified a Constitutional Convention to revise portions which might today be deemed "obsolete".

Change is in the wind, but what does Pi say? Well we have looked at the year 2020 (or 2020.05) which says something to be sure, but what else? The Founding Year of 1776 + 233 gives (as previously stated) 2009. As also noted, if one adds 11 on to this (from above, did you remember it?) we arrive at 2020. However, the US Constitution was promulgated in 1787 and if we go forward 233 years from this date we arrive at (drum roll please!) ... 2020! Something VERY big regarding this document is in the wind in other words! (COVID is huge!)

One of the things which Americans hold dear is the Office of the Presidency. Some 44 people have held the Office of the President with Barack Obama being the most recent. Wait ... no! There are only

43 people if one counts them one by one as Grover Cleveland was both the 22nd and 24th President which muddies things a little bit.

If one looks at the Pi calculations I noted above (derived from the various mathematical roots of 3.1416) we see that the square root less the 4th root is 177-133 or 44. Yes, maybe I am reaching a bit here, but there is so much in the simple derivatives (to use a word which so many people find disgusting these days!) from Daniel that perhaps we can continue to extrapolate some more: especially as all of this fits so well with the future of the US Constitution.

We are at the 43rd President (in reality) which means that as Mr. Obama must step down in early 2017 the next President (Hillary Clinton?) must be the 44th. Would she be the first woman President; and possibly the last one of all? If there is a major change in the US Constitution in 2020 (ie just before the normally scheduled quadrennial election scheduled for that Fall) then the 44 number from the Pi cycle would be accurate.

So, yet again we have ANOTHER indicator that something big is brewing in just a few years. If I had to guess about all of this I would say that the very dangerous financial crisis which looks to be brewing as we head into the year 2016 (an election year to boot), will leave an economy which is pretty well dependent on ever larger amounts of credit, in desperate straits. As I have mentioned in the newsletter, it may well be that an attempted take down of the US existing power structure might be on the cards as well!! Yes, and this is all in the Book of Revelation and, by and by, I shall get to it and detail what I think will happen; always assuming that Pi and the End Times theory are correct. Oh, Yes! In looking at how one derives future dates which fit into 2032 which is a seminal year for Mr. Armstrong, we can see that this can be derived from what I have written a few paragraphs above and also in (yet again!) another manner. Armstrong gives the clear implication that various economic cycles (i.e. the 1981 interest rate hikes by then

Fed Chairman Paul Volcker plus 51 gives 2032) can be extrapolated forward to arrive at 2032 and then 2037.

I have to concur with what he is saying as US history going forward will be, in the main, one of economics and the unwinding of really horrendous derivative bubbles. So therefore, we go back to the secondary recession of 2010 and add the 22 year "Half an Hour" cycle and we get ... 2032!! So, this fits as well. The 2037 number can be simply derived by taking the 2015 year (looming larger and ever more important) and adding this 22 number yet again i.e. 2015+ 22= 2037! I find it amazing how all of these things simply seem to just keep coming together!

Oh, all right: let's have one more bit of analysis then! Let's look at an institution which has dominated the US for just over 100 years: coming into being as what many regards as a very sinister Christmas present in the year 1913. Is this a most wicked group of people (the twelve members of the Board of Governors, only seven of whom can vote at any one time) who can do whatever they want, to what might be the obvious detriment of the American people? I take no position on this although I will discuss this as does the Book of Revelation which I will analyses in depth in a later segment of this book. However, we have just had the Fed's centenary this past Christmas and what happens now? Well six Pi Cycles come to 18.85 years and if one adds these to Christmas 2013, guess what we come up with?? Yep! It is our new friend the year 2032! So, do we have a terrible problem with the economy (possibly with the cashless society which is also coming quite soon now – yes, Revelation again) which leads some desperate reformers to abolish what many people regard as a most venal institution? I think it quite probable.

So, within the now nailed down parameters of 2010/2032, we shall clearly in the fullness of time be able to see smaller, but no less significant, sub-cycles. The major one, as far as I am concerned, lies in the interpretation of Revelation Chapter 12 and the "war in heaven"/rebellion analysis which I was making an informed guess about in the newsletter. This is led by what appears to be conservative Christians and we have to wonder about the US Constitution if this uprising takes place. Well, the US Founding Document was written in 1787 and if we add the now familiar 233 to this we arrive at the year 2020. This, interestingly enough is an exact Pi cycle number as noted, and so I feel reasonably confident that it has a great deal of merit in Pi cycle analysis in general.

So, what I am saying is that this venerable US document will probably be changed by either the winning side in the initial rebellion, slightly, or rather dramatically so when the beast and its minions recapture control of the US.

Have I let the cat out of the bag? I probably have but let's let you stew and ponder this one. The South shall rise again indeed!!

SEGMENT TWO

CHAPTER ONE

◆ ◆ ◆ ◆ ◆

US EYES CANADA (MUNCH,
MUNCH ... CHOMP, CHOMP?)

Aand to that we might wonder if there is enough Pepto-Bismol in the world to correct the sort of stomach distress which such a meal would cause! In all seriousness we can note that throughout its history, the US has eyed Canada and its vast open spaces and immense natural resources. Chief among these, initially, must be oil, as seen in the Alberta Tar Sands which are supposed to hold (Wikipedia - http://en.wikipedia.org/wiki/Oil_sands) some 1.75 trillion barrels of oil (or equivalent). To put this in understandable terms, if all of this could be mined (probably an accurate way to describe how this resource is currently being exploited), it would probably supply the energy/fuel demands for the entire of North America for three centuries. If a much smaller portion of all of this could be extracted before it was deemed that nothing more could be taken, we are still looking at meeting North American demands for the rest of this century! Given that Saudi Arabia may well be running out of what can be extracted profitably (not to mention the military threats and so forth endemic in that region of the globe), Alberta is literally a gift from God. In passing, I should note that other estimates (which I have used in my newsletters on this subject) put the Tar Sands deposits at about equal to all of the remaining crude oil deposits (ie non-Tar Sands type of oil) in the rest of the world!

Anyway you put it, there is a terrific supply of oil in the remote northern reaches of Alberta. At present writing (May 3, 2014) we can say that most of this resource should probably be headed towards the US (and the Texas refineries) via the long-delayed Keystone XL pipeline at some point in the future. However it is not, and with very real problems in the Middle East never seeming to go away (since the 1973 Arab-Israeli War and the ensuing embargo in 1974), it stands to reason that oil producers in the US are already casting covetous eyes on the region. Americans have long had the feeling (it used to be referred to as Manifest Destiny many years ago) that they had natural rights to the entire Continent of North America. When I studied this at school (just about fifty years ago – so it really is not a new idea!) I came to the conclusion that in the aftermath of their Revolutionary War there was not a lot of good feelings in the new USA towards Great Britain and the rest of its global empire. As Canada (not yet to be a nation for many decades to come) was part of this empire, it was (I suppose) only natural to the new capital of Washington that some sort vast nation comprising North America should come into being. However, the new United States probably had more than enough on its nascent plate without worrying about why inhabitants of Upper and Lower Canada did not shuck off the British crown and join up with the former colonies to the south.

This feeling has not gone away in the least in the past two hundred odd years and every now and again, somebody in the Corridors of Power in Washington gets it in their head that the ongoing economic demands for the oft-sputtering US economy would be much more easily addressed if the two major countries on this continent were joined.

I suppose that one cannot forget "little" Mexico, and in the arcane world of NAFTA any sort of continent-wide land grab by its major partner must include Mexico. In my newsletters, I wrote about this possibility last November (2013) and the fact that Hillary Clinton (in my mind the leading candidate to assume the Office of the US Presidency in the 2024 elections) also seems to have this under consideration. I have followed this woman ever since her husband, Bill Clinton, won election to this office in 1992. She is, in my mind, extraordinarily intelligent and seems to have a strong lust for power to accomplish her own objectives. My sense is that she grew up in an era (essentially my own) when women were regarded as little more than an appendage to their husbands and were treated as such.

Understand that I am not going to write on this particular sociological subject as it falls outside the purview of this book, but I do note it in passing and I am sure that Hillary wanted to do something about it. Well, if she wins in 2016 (and I believe that she will) then she will have reached the summit of what a US woman can aspire to and will govern accordingly. That would be for domestic politics, but she has shown that she has a strong aptitude for international politics in what (to borrow an old Soviet term) Americans would regard as the "Near Abroad": namely Mexico and Canada). Just to highlight, below, what I wrote in the newsletters, Clinton has made strong reference to a new way that NAFTA would work together in a Clinton Presidency. Latinos in Los Angeles, where she gave the speech, apparently loved hearing from her in any event and there was no bad feedback from what she said. In March this year (2014) she made a visit to Calgary and said very little of consequence to an overflow audience there, but then there was the point which everyone missed: why she was there at all. Keep in mind that she visited a city where Canadian Prime Minister Harper comes from (his federal riding is located there) and so did then Premier Alison Redford (before she resigned suddenly in a spending scandal). A neighboring riding (my own actually), is called home by the leader of the Wildrose provincial opposition party, Danielle Smith. In this Albertan city we also find the headquarters of many Canadian oil companies as well. So Hillary, in her very intelligent way of feeling something out, has probably made some good contacts for her presumed time at 1600 Pennsylvania Avenue. She has a plan in mind for North America and of that I am certain.

OK, here is the comment Clinton made in Los Angeles back last November which I was referring to above. I have truncated the actual article (taken from The Japan Times, of all newspapers. What happened to general US coverage I wonder?). Note where I have highlighted. Now if we add this to her coming to Calgary, we can say that she definitely has something in mind for North America and that, clearly, includes Canada. I am guessing here, but I think it says that she wants US industrial capability combined with lots of cheap Mexican labour all powered by nearly limitless Canadian natural resources. Here it is:- In L.A., supporters of a 2016 Clinton run ready to get on board early The Washington Post http://www.japantimes. co.jp/news/2013/11/10/world/in-l-a-supporters-of-a-2016-clinton-run-ready-to-get-on-board-early/Nov 10, 2013 http://www.addthis. com/bookmark.php?v=300&pubid=jtimes

- LOS ANGELES – Hillary Rodham Clinton stood on another stage, facing another overflowing ballroom. This time the locale was the University of Southern California, where the elegant Town and Gown hall was jammed to capacity Saturday morning with more than 400 members of the country's Latino political and business elite. The agenda: honoring the former secretary of state for her role in inspiring the creation of the Mexican American Leadership Initiative, a group of prominent Latinos who support philanthropic projects in Mexico and promote what Clinton called "a shared future" between the two nations.

Now let's have a look at what Clinton did (according to the newspapers up here) on her trip to Calgary. This what I sent out in my newsletter. The thinking is still quite valid in my view:-

---

"I have postponed writing on this woman (again) until after her visit to Calgary on March 6. It looks like I needn't have bothered as she came to the Telus Centre in Calgary and spoke before 2,500 curious souls for all of 24 minutes. The major question for Albertans is what is going to happen in Washington (either before or after a

President Clinton takes office) regarding the Keystone pipeline which would take the Tar Sands oil to Texas for refining and selling.

"At least six times our Alberta Premier (roughly equivalent of a US State Governor) has visited Washington to plead her case for the Obama Administration to drop its opposition to this venture, and every time Alberta has come away empty handed. It therefore seems clear that nothing is going to be done during the tenure of a President Obama. All Hillary had to say at the Telus Centre was that there was a process going on and that she could not comment any further! "This was very disappointing for both Premier Redford and Albertans in general. As if to rub in that fact that she had little to say, she commented on the igloo building programme at Calgary University (yes, it seems that there is one!) and made reference that while she was a great friend of Canadians in general, she did not know much about Calgary! "Oh yes, she made the seemingly obligatory comments equating Russian President Putin to Adolph Hitler. In other words she was careful to say nothing at all which could be used against her as she plods along towards what seems to be a certain victory as Democrat candidate for US President in 2024 (ie the Democratic Party 'process'), and then to be a most formidable candidate in the following general election. "It looks like she has GOP strategists worried as all they can apparently come up with to counter her immense popularity is a series of questions about her age and general health. I seem to recall that at the start of Ronald Reagan's first term, similar worries were expressed by the Democrats! Ah, well what goes around comes around!

"Back to Mrs. Clinton's Calgary visit if I may. Surely she did not come to Calgary to complement the local university's igloo building programme! She may have come to see where a possible challenger, Ted Cruz, was born (which makes me wonder how the GOP is going to explain this one given their insistence that Barack Obama is ineligible for the office he holds as he was supposedly born in Kenya). "As Mr. Cruz was born here, perhaps he has some supporters and perhaps she wanted to see who they are and what sorts of threats they may represent to her. What, and this makes more sense as she is a very clever planner, she may actually have done is to meet the overall movers and shakers here. What movers and shakers you ask? "Well, Calgary is the oil capital of the most important oil patch on the planet (yes, the Tar Sands count!) and this is where oil movers and shakers hang out. So, the real question is whom did she see, visit and talk to (make deals with??) before she made her vacuous speech on Thursday morning? Enquiring minds want to know! "So what can we glean from this meet-and-greet behind the scenes supposition? I think Hillary knows full well about the overall situation in the world, both from the prospects of energy and food security. Keep in mind the vast Ukrainian grain growing areas. "It seems clear (and I shall discuss this next week on a Ukrainian update which one reader asked me to do) that she is being regularly updated on these two situations and is planning accordingly. She has already (although this ethnic grouping was probably already in her pocket) made comments to the Los Angeles Latino community about bringing the three NAFTA nations together which are essentially code words for bringing into the United States a whole panoply of skills from Mexico. "This influx (and consequent increase in US industrial production) would be fueled by Canadian (Albertan) oil as we have discussed previously. Her trip to Calgary is to line up Canadian oil magnates and also politicians. Keep in mind that Prime Minister Harper comes from a Calgary district and represents it in Parliament in Ottawa. Alberta Premier Redford also comes from the Calgary area and so the number of influential people Hillary may have gotten to meet is quite substantial. "She plans well. Of that there can be no doubt. She was US Secretary of State and therefore knows a very great deal about how things are transacted around the world. The interesting question is whether she advised President Obama on what might happen in the Ukraine and how this could be moved to US advantage. "As an aside here, just how strong is the US anyhow? From what I am reading in RT.com it seems that President Putin looks to be climbing down on the issue of Russians in the Eastern portion of the Ukraine concerning their security and may even be considering something similar in the Crimea. "I cannot believe this to be frank, but the fact that he is doing next to nothing while the new ad-hoc government in Kiev is flexing its muscles is astonishing. Does Hillary know the man that well and that when push comes to shove, he can be told (in effect) what to do? Such a woman, as US President (especially when she has been recently described as a very tough person), would be a formidable opponent throughout the world. "There is, of course, the problem of getting by the US election process in 2016 and 2020 but I suspect she is not unduly concerned. If she has had the opportunity to talk with oil moguls in her Calgary trip, then I would imagine it may be a fairly simple process to offer them "considerations" in return for them supporting what she has in mind for the period 2017-2021 (at least!). "Now, if she can do this to Albertan oil executives, then how much further pressure can she bring on US executives? My guess is that many Mexican workers, on goodness-knows what sorts of visas, will come to the US. What Hillary is probably telling these business interests is that, for them, the clear implication is that huge new profits can be reaped with lower fringe benefits (think health care here?) at the very least. "Hillary would be a powerful incentive for these people to support her in 2024 and I am sure she knows all about this. Find their weak spot and hit at it. It will work well in the US and almost certainly with the oil people in Alberta. Something along these lines is her probable plan and while I do not like her, I must commend her ruthlessness in planning this far ahead. "So, what now, assuming all of this supposition on my part is correct? Well I am not a confidant of Mrs. Clinton (clearly!), but I would look for more strategic planning depending on what goodies the US State Department can cook up (i.e. where is the next Ukraine). She most probably has good contacts in that department and will use them unceasingly. "The GOP also knows all of this and it might be behind the recent stories that Hillary is either 'too old' to serve or has possible health problems, as referenced above. If this is the best they can do, there is little chance they will succeed in a little under three years against an opponent as formidable as Mrs. Clinton!"

(There! The end of a long paste about Mrs. Clinton)

Well, have a look at all of this and be prepared (for right or wrong) for America's first woman president and its 44-45th (numerically speaking) overall. She will be very calculating, exceptionally well informed, and has a very good idea of what she wants to do because she has already worked it all out in that wonderful mind of hers! I do not believe that she will be that relenting to her opponents (and the GOP may regret taking her on with various issues). In fact I would even go as far as to say that the GOP is probably wondering who they can put up as their candidate against her and are probably crying in their beer over the fact that she is a Democrat! Such is the life in America's political Capitol! However, she is but one cog in the wheel on the whole, emotive, subject of a US/Canada merger (as it has been referred to in the newsletter). So, let us assume that Hillary will be the 44-45th numerical President which means she will be a prime mover (if not THE prime mover) on this sorry subject. However, for there to be any movement on this, there must be an underlying base of economic fundamentals or else nothing at all would be happening – and this chapter in the book would not even have been considered much less written!

SEGMENT TWO

CHAPTER TWO

✦✦✦✦✦

STILL MUNCHING AND CHOMPING
(WHO ELSE BESIDES HILLARY HAS
THIS ENORMOUS APPETITE?)

I spent almost the entire of Chapter One in this Segment looking at the very dangerous, highly intelligent, and probably soon-to-be leader of the United States and how, I believe, she is looking at a take-over of Canada. Speaking as a Canadian, I am most concerned with how the wheels in her head will grind ever finer and finer as she becomes ever more at home in her new office in 2025.

However, that is roughly eight years from now. That is a long time in the forecasting business and given that we still have a War Cycle (thank you Marty Armstrong for this, unfortunately as accurate as ever) to stagger through followed by a major bond market debacle about eighteen months from now, there must be something that the USA-phoebes in Canada have to be more concerned about. Regrettably there is. I should probably wait until this book's segment on oil before going into this more fully, but in order to let you see what I am worried about in terms of Canada's sovereignty, I had better explain the principle of "backwardation" now. This is very counter-intuitive (typical of today's markets I suppose) but it is accurate in any event. I shall leave aside the mathematics of time decay on prices and so forth and stick with the very basics.

Let us look at crude oil markets as we currently see them today, and which can be verified on the COMEX markets which trade in Chicago. Let us say the month which sees all of the action is June (which it is at current writing; May 4, 2014) and standard delivery crude is trading at $ 99.50 per 42 US gallon barrel. Well, not all of the trading takes place in this "front month" (as it is called). Traders can hedge and speculate in a wide range of dates, going out to December 2022, so it is quite a liquid market: what is called "deep". Oil trades for a final settlement price (the final price in other words) each trading day. The difference between the price quotes of, say, June and July is what interests us in looking at the phenomenon of backwardation. In the final analysis, this tells us a lot about the availability of crude and how this will affect Canada. Let me scream this out in no uncertain terms: A BACKWARDATED MARKET IS ONE WHICH CALLS FOR SHORTAGES GOING FORWARD. THAT'S RIGHT – SHORTAGES AND NOT SURPLUSES!! OK Gerry, you have made your point. Now what DOES this mean??

So, we see the June contract price is $ 99.50 and backwardation price structure tells us that the July price is $ 99.00 (ie 50 cents LESS than the June price!). Yes, you read that right. July price is lower then the June price and, because this so-called backwardation goes all the way out to December 2022 we see the price there at $ 80.13 which is a DISCOUNT of about 19.5% to June 2014. So, why is this? Why is it that a commodity which is in short supply sees its price become cheaper the further out one goes? At the very least such would seem to be counter-intuitive, but that is the way it is. Again, WHY IS THIS SO?? Alright, think along the following lines. If you believe, for whatever reason, that oil is in short supply what do you do? Well, if I were an end/final user, I would make sure that I had all that I could handle. I would make sure that every storage container I possessed was full to the brim with real, useable, product which I would have to sell to my customers. This means that in the next few months, having the feeling that a shortage could be coming, I would be buying some of my requirements for, say, the next six months today and storing them immediately. This would have the effect of bidding up the contracts for the next few months at the expense of contracts for the end of the year or even over the next few years. Therefore, we would see the backwardation develop which we are seeing so extensively in the crude oil markets today. Again - backwardation is seen when the price of two monthly contracts, in our case June and July 2014, sees June at $ 99.50 and July at $ 99.00. Buying, possibly made greater by overall fears of a gathering shortage, would be concentrated in the next few months at the expense of, say, Christmas contract. More buying now and less at Christmas means the price now will be higher than in the December (Christmas) contract. We should also not forget the problem that in dealing with commodities, there is the storage factor. If everyone wants to buy now and hold the commodity until needed, this will also bid up the storage price as this legitimate cost must be added to the final price for the consumer. Therefore, if you wish to buy now and avoid paying a hefty storage fee to someone who has bought a contract for July, or August, or ... whenever, you must compensate that person. We see this in the backward dated price curve (learning the lingo now are we?!). So, if you buy a contract for December 2022 with the intent of sitting on it for roughly eight and a half years, you will be compensated an amazing (as already noted) 19.5% for your costs. Of course, if you are a speculative player and say "Right! Oil is going MUCH higher and this is the cheapest I can get, I will buy and hold". If oil goes to $ 200 in December 2022, then I would sell my contract at $ 200 and make the spread that was available from today, plus my 19.5%. I will be rich! Yes, you will be assuming that the organized markets hold together long enough for your contract to mature and for you to take your healthy profits and run away to somewhere nice to live your life of ease! We might also say with a 19.5% discount that perhaps the market is saying something like "Eight and a half years is a long time to wait for my profits. What happens if the rising oil price causes a really devastating recession which would cause the price of oil to fall a very long way? It is likely that you will see something like this happen so why are you taking such a huge risk?". The answer is that the market feels that a 19.5% discount is probably about right for the risk you are taking.

However, that is all trader talk. This chapter is about a US takeover of Canada (which has been called "The Merger" by myself and others) and so what can we say about the real purpose of this takeover? I say (and there must be a LOT of people in official

Washington think tanks agreeing with this) that with growing oil shortages (they ain't making the stuff anymore!) the major consumers in the United States may be sick of all of the machinations in the Middle East. They want stability in their sources of supply. Let me put this all as plainly as I can. Backwardation means shortages of crude going forward as we have seen. THE US IS SHORT OF OIL. CANADA (ALBERTA) HAS PLENTY OF THE STUFF. THE US NEEDS THIS. IT WILL TRY TO GET IT VIA A GIANT CANADA/US MERGER IS MY ARGUMENT. They, the USA consumers, note that Britain and Argentina are at loggerheads over what could be an enormous find in the remote Falkland Islands. Britain is so anxious to hang on to this (the Falklands being a British colony and voting by a very wide margin to retain this status in a referendum about a year ago) that London is building a major airstrip on the very remote Island of St. Helena which could be used, at short notice, to fly military equipment to the Mt. Pleasant airbase in the Falklands. St. Helena island is also a British colony.

We can see also that China is gazing, eyeball-to-eyeball, with the Philippines, Viet Nam, and Japan over various claims in the huge South China Sea. While I have not heard that much about this in the last little while, oil (what else?) was mentioned as a prime motivator for all of this possible hostility. There is much aggravation in the world over oil, so does it not make sense that people at the head of Exxon and the like would much appreciate a breather from all of this and look at nice, quiet, Canada (and Alberta in particular)! And this is what I have been leading up to! Canada (and the Province of Alberta in particular which has, for some reason, just about all of the Continent's Tar Sands deposits) is a nice quiet pace where nothing ever seems to happen. The quasi-separatist portion of Canada is located in Quebec and is thousands of miles away. In contrast, quiet Alberta has a pro-business attitude and a flat tax which everyone on the Continent seems to envy. Surely, if the US oil majors wanted an easy set of oil production quotas, then this would be the place. What I think happened is that a lot of people, looking at the mess of global oil supplies (rapidly contracting as can be seen in the backwardation phenomenon), decided that a Canada/US merger was definitely in the interests of Washington's energy planning. So, given this we came to a story in the Washington Times. There was, earlier this year (2014), an interesting comment in the Washington Times which tends to be somewhat (as I understand it) to the right of center in US political discourse. Anyhow it ran what I think has to be what is referred to as a "Merger" trial balloon in the form of an article from the Canadian equivalent publication, the National Post. The story, which was not well put together as regards facts and the like, was all about how the US and Canada should, finally, come together as one political unit under one flag in North America. I wrote on this "Merger" idea in the newsletter at some length and I wish to include this now. It reads:-

"No, I am not referring to some sort of mega-corporate get together, but rather something I have noted in the past and which is rearing its ugly head once again: a possible takeover of Canada by the United States. This seems to come to the fore every few years and now it might even be some sort of political takeover by neo-cons or a play for the biggest oil reserves on the planet: the Alberta Tar Sands. "I have written about the possibilities of Alberta and British Columbia looking to go it alone if there were real problems stirring in Ottawa (Canada's capital) over energy mining (for that is how the Tar Sands are effectively developed), and in that essay I wondered about the US authorities allowing such a conglomerate to exist for anything but a short period of time. (NOTE: I am going to look at this in much more detail in the next chapter - Gerry). "Since I wrote that series of updates, we have seen (and heard on Slovak radio) some very good comments by the redoubtable Paul Craig Roberts to the effect that the neo-cons pretty well control the decision making process in Washington and that their goal is total global hegemony where their word is, essentially, global law. "To get this operation into full swing, Washington would have to have access to unlimited amounts of energy. This would be required to ensure that Washington could do whatever it wanted on a global scale (probably militarily) with no worries about this critical energy component. "As Washington grabbed more and more resources on its apparent never ending hunt, the rest of the world would be squeezed badly: think China here. So, am I having some sort of nightmare as I write this? No, I do not think so. Have a look at the following. http://www.washingtontimes.com/news/2014/mar/23/border-buddies-author-touts-merger-between-the-uni/?page=all#pagebreak

"At about the same time that Mr. Roberts was making his comments about the sheer evil which seems to be running Washington, we see this article trotted out in a rather right-wing newspaper on the subject of 'Border buddies: A Merger between the United States and Canada' with a sub-headline reading "Visionary writer starts with a 'thought experiment' ". "It smells to me like the proverbial trial balloon. If we examine some of the comments in the article we also see that it would be a resource grab of the largest dimension imaginable. For example: -

"I wanted to attack the Canadian establishment and say, 'Wake up, there is [a merger] underway, let's manage it to our benefit,' and to attack American ignorance about Canada," she said.

Note the words: 'Wake up, there is a merger underway'. Further on in the article we see:- "The North American colossus would control more oil, water, arable land and resources than any other country, all protected by the world's most powerful military".

And we have (as this newspaper article is written by a Canadian who apparently contributes to the National Post in Canada) something from an American writing for a foreign policy journal called "Suffragio":-

"Kevin Lees, founder and editor of the foreign policy journal Suffragio, said the United States can benefit easily and immediately from 'low-hanging fruit' in Canada".

That pretty well concludes my direct comments on this article, although I do give it later on in this chapter for your complete understanding.

So, we see (if we take all of these things together) a resource grab. The three comments noted above talk about "a merger being underway"; "more oil, land, and water than anybody else"; and "low hanging fruit". I think if I have misinterpreted all of this, that hopefully the reader may forgive me. If it walks like a duck and quacks like a duck, then it probably is a duck! Let's come back to this resource angle a little later on if I may. If one re-reads the story from the Washington Times, we see that such a merger would add thirteen stars to the new US flag as this number of provinces would become states. Well, Canada does not have thirteen provinces. It has ten provinces and three territories: the Yukon, Northwest Territories, and Nunavut. To just take one of these, the Yukon, (which I happen to be familiar with) we see that it has about 33,000 people living there, about 75% of which are in the territorial capital of Whitehorse. The territory is about 186,000 square miles in area which would make it appreciably larger than most US states. Still, I do not see a huge land area, mostly uninhabited, being admitted to the US as a state with only 33,000 people! Not many people live "Up North" in Canada as a whole and to create three new states from ice and snow is not going to work at all! However, the author seems to think this will be the case even though she wishes to consign Canada's problem child of Quebec to the status of Puerto Rico: a territory. So, the author wishes to deprive nearly 8 million Canadian citizens of the right to vote, on the basis of ethnicity and have no representation in a Congress in Washington, while allowing a few score thousand to have full such rights (which other US flyweights such as Guam do not!).

Wonderful thinking, and if the rest of what she writes about is of the same quality then perhaps we could end this lengthy essay here and now! Look at her math. There are (she says, as noted) thirteen provinces (ten in reality) which will obtain starts on the revised US flag, but with only nine provinces in her math (ie the ten we have now less Quebec makes nine) I wonder about the author.

However, she did us a service is addressing this issue. The US authorities have shown themselves to be most amenable to a takeover of Canada, most recently in terms of "trade benefits" for both sides. In the late 1950s, when the US was rapidly expanding its economy after WW 2, there was an initiative called "NAWAPA" which was short for North American Water And Power Alliance. Basically, for the large amount (back then with the rather limited capital markets versus what we have today) of $ 100 billion, the US wanted to make Canada what would have been the ultimate hewer of wood and drawer of water. The interior of British Columbia was to be filled with what would have been a giant lake for US irrigation purposes and possibly a reserve for western hydro-electric dams. Northern Quebec was to be a huge supplier of hydro-power for the industrial US north-east, and on and on it went. Mercifully, nothing came of this – I am guessing because of the estimated expense. Still, it gave us an indication of what the thinking was in the Corridors of Power in Washington.

Not much else was done on this issue until the middle to late 1960s when the issue rose again. Then we saw the idea of a commonality of interests which would have resulted in Washington enticing the western provinces (excluding BC for some reason) into the US, with all of the staggering resources which were available. Ontario was left out of this equation (despite the industrial capacity of the place) which laid bare the idea of a raw materials grab. At that time, interestingly enough, Quebec did not seem to figure in Washington's economic calculus and on the maps of the proposed new North America it was either marked "independent" or "other". Again, with the general disgust over the Viet Nam conflict, nothing became of this. The US is now trying the NAFTA idea to rope Canada and Mexico into the proposed North American Union and at one point maybe ten years ago we had then President Bush come up with the idea of a common North American currency, somewhat lamely called the "Amero".

The way this was to be set up was little better than a scam of immense proportions, and when this became generally realised the idea was dropped. However, I am getting ahead of myself a bit here. In 1990, the Quebec issue and the infamous Meech lake Accord reared its ugly head in Canada once again and once more I started to see syndicated editorials in major US newspapers about how the US could again absorb Canada. This time we were looking at blocs of provinces which would be absorbed into a common union. Here we were to see BC as one state; the prairie provinces would form another; Ontario and then Quebec would be two others (no leaving Quebec out this time given the extraordinary importance of Quebec hydro-power to the northeastern States!); and then no one could figure out what to do with Canada's welfare provinces "Down East". This also went nowhere fast and I never saw this raised again, at least in this format.

Now we see the latest incarnation of all of this. It is, again, a play for natural resources and this might finally see all of the marbles on the table. Unlike the days of NAWAPA and other attempts going forward, there are things which the now developed financial markets are telling us about energy supplies going forward – globally this time. I have written about all of what follows before, but I wish to do so again as I desire, strongly, to emphasise the global positioning in oil. Again, we note that COMEX is seeing a backwardation (mercifully it does not seem to be growing the further out the time curve one goes, although I am worried when I see a near term widening/getting bigger of this critical measure) of prices for as far out as one cares to go. In terms of tradeable contracts, we can go to 2022 and still the stubborn message is that oil is in short supply (relative to increasing global demand) and this is not going to change one iota. One new thing I can add here is the degree of demand from US trading houses. As a former trader speaking here, I can say that there is one thing which I pay the strictest attention to and that is market bias. Recently, there have been events happening which should have spelled that there was (for the short term at least) an oversupply of oil which should have pushed the price down fairly sharply. The biggest of these was the ongoing belief that the Chinese economy (which is the second biggest user of oil in the world – after, of course, the United States) was weakening, possibly dramatically so. Under normal circumstances this should have seen a large crude sell off but not this time! The spot price fell from $ 103 to $ 97.50 or so and then bounced dramatically to recoup nearly all of this. We are told that there was a big demand for WTI (West Texas Intermediate) and whereas this is worth knowing as the reason for the bounce, it is still only one part of the equation for oil pricing.

A major slowdown in China would mean a sustained drop in prices as a lot of oil which used to go to China would have been without a home (translation – would be sold on the futures markets at a discount). The China story should have been enduring as it is HUGE, and yet the Cushing supply (for WTI) seemed to rule the roost. In short, whenever there is a dip in oil prices for whatever reason, there are a LOT of buyers suddenly coming into focus. The bias is therefore for oil to be actively sought after whatever the news and possible changes are and how they affect macro-considerations. The demand from sources which actually use the stuff is strong and this does not include trading houses and banks (keep in mind the trader "God", whom I believe is still around - see the end of the book) which will have noticed the price bias and be actively be on the bids as prices see occasional falls. Let me emphasise this. Backwardation says that there shortages for as far out as you care to go. This is serious for a major consumer such as the US. Price bias says that there are LOTS of fresh buyers at virtually every major price level. Why on earth should you NOT be a buyer given these considerations, either speculatively or for "real" purposes? Speaking as a trader, you should and we shall continue to see this idea I think. Now that I have been writing on this, let me draw it all into the theme for this series of letters: a Canada/US merger.

The redoubtable Paul Craig Roberts has been writing and giving radio interviews about how the very right-wing neo-cons have taken power in Washington (behind the scenes) and no matter who is temporarily in the White House their agenda is the only one which matters. Roberts says that they want nothing less than American hegemony across the globe and are so determined to have this (for what he calls "the exceptional people") that they are risking nuclear war with Russia – which, they believe is winnable. OK, so much for the political aspects of what Washington DC may or may not want, the idea which I have is that in order to gain this global supremacy the US must have unfettered access to a full set of industrial components such as hydro-electric power, raw materials, and of course oil. According to Wikipedia the Tar Sands (yep, back to that again!) has as much oil as the rest of the world has in conventional reserves: some 1.6 trillion barrels. For an avaricious oil major, this is a prize of world-beating proportions and must be secured before it may be sold off to Chinese interests, or (heaven forbid) the energy starved EU which, be it remembered, is trying to conclude a trade pact with Canada (the long delayed CETA accord). Neo-cons would desire this treasure and they would want it before a CETA-inspired Shell oil company (as an example) grabs a portion of it. It seems to be a question of control.

So, with all of the cards now in the process of being laid on the table, we see that global demand for energy (in the face of ever expanding industrial production) is now going to soar. Longer term planners will have noticed this and we see that Manitoba and BC hydros will be a very important component of what Washington feels the level of US economy should be performing at. The question is how to access this as it would take a pliant government in Ottawa to be able to get this done. My guess, with elections scheduled for next year in Canada (federal elections), that the neo-cons would want a Conservative government (such as the one we have today under Prime Minister Harper) who could be pressured into presenting something along these lines to the Canadian public. If Washington were to wait too long, then we might have a Liberal Government under Justin Trudeau, the son of the (late) popular Pierre Elliot Trudeau who ruled the roost as PM for many years starting in 1968. Justin's Liberals have a decent lead over Harper as at this current writing and I do not believe that as a new PM (should he win next year) he would like to make a monumental decision such as The Merger, at least immediately. Remembering his father as I do, we might say that Justin would not like the idea anyhow. So, with time short (in my estimation), Washington has to act.

Again, referring back to the newsletter:-

"If we consider again the Washington Times article, a couple of lines stand out for me. If we return to the US foreign policy journal Suffragio we see a very blunt comment- "The good news is that policymakers on both sides of the border are very much considering those ideas," he said.

"So, was there some really strong talk at the recent NAFTA summit in Mexico then? If Suffragio makes this sort of very unambiguous comment, then I am inclined to think that there was. Following this summit and the comments about neo-con supremacy in Washington, an article such as what we are seeing backed up with a lot of behind the scenes comments is probably the next step in this most audacious plan. "Will Harper go along with this at all, knowing that it would not be popular across the country? If he is looking to leave some sort of legacy then he might, knowing full well that there would not be the force in Parliament to counter his wishes, although there would probably be some nasty infighting on the entire issue in his Cabinet. "What Harper will probably have to do is to have some sort of Continent-wide decision making authority with this grouping approved within Canada, so that the border (in theory at least) still remains intact. This would provide a fig-leaf for Liberal and NDP supporters (Canada's major opposition parties) to claim that nothing really has changed. "We could still see a Canadian Dollar in use (much as several countries in the EU still use their own currencies – Sweden, Denmark, the UK, and Poland come to mind) in an expanded North American condominium such as what we are discussing. That too would be for show and nothing else and would be kept in a very tight band in trading against the powerful US$.

"All right, we have looked at oil to the point of exhaustion but there is another element which we have to have a quick look at and that is ... water. Canada has huge reserves of this most precious resource, most of it locked away in the remote territories of Nunavut and the NWT. "Under the terms of NAFTA, US interests cannot get at this water unless Canada declares it to be a commodity which can be exploited fully within the country. Then US interests can claim that under the trade treaty they have a perfect right to climb on board this particular gravy train and exploit it to a fare-the-well. "It is probably this fear that has kept water away from parched US States as there is still a very strong belief that the US has squandered its own very substantial resources in this area, and why should the US be given access to anything more to waste yet again? "We must examine this belief and I think that it might be very well behind what the neo-cons are trying to accomplish. A US/Canada under NAFTA means that Canada's water is safe despite more and more grumbling about how the US farm belt, (especially under the dubious heading of global warming) needs this water urgently. "A Canada is which is part of the US to the extent of having its own stars on the US flag would be quite a different matter. As a single country the water would be up for grabs. In some respects one can see that a long-term thinking neo-con would be saying that, by and large (with CETA exceptions noted briefly above), the US can get the oil it needs from Canada when it wants it. "It is only the political control which is missing. However, what is the point of having all of the oil one can ever use if the means to grow crops in the US is to be impaired? Therefore, if the idea of having an economically solid US economy is at the base of overseas expansion, the water situation MUST be taken care of. It must also be eliminated as a worry as soon as possible in my view, especially with all of the headlines about a 500 year drought in California being bandied about!

"Well, let's close off this rather lengthy series on a subject which may never come to pass (perhaps the US undergoes financial collapse, not impossible given the Pi and Armstrong analyses, before it can make eyes at Canada – however that is done these days!). What do I think of all of this? Do I approve? "No, manifestly I do not as there are simply too many negatives for Canada in such an arrangement. If you wish, it is an 'agreement' between two partners who are NOT equal. Where is the benefit for Canadians? Do we get to go and live in retirement in Arizona without any visa nonsense (Wow! What's that really worth anyway)? "Do we get (depending on where you live, of course) to send representatives to Washington's Congress where they will be dwarfed by the large numbers of Congressmen from US States? (probably 9:1 ratio against Canadians. Where is the benefit in that?). Adopting the IRS Tax Code?? Definitely I would say 'Where's the benefit'? "I also worry about medicare (being an official senior citizen now!) here. It is self-funding in Alberta because of the huge oil revenues but what happens after a takeover? Are oldies like myself to be 'grandfathered' in (ha!ha!)? I can probably go on and on with this as you can imagine, but to what extent? "If people like those in DC (who most probably want this sort of thing to occur) have their eyes set on money and power and how fast it can be accumulated, then they will not give the proverbial Tinker's Dam about the annoying complications which will be sure to arise. Devil take the hindmost indeed! Do I approve of such a merger? "As stated before, I certainly do NOT. However, that being said, will it happen? With deep regret I believe that it will. How can I say that? Simply this – look at how a trader would regard everything I have presented. A good trader will assess the trend overall and go with it. From the days of NAWAPA to today's resource starved world, this trend is getting stronger. Therefore (shudder) it WILL happen and probably a lot sooner then people think. "Think on this, especially my Canadian readers". Gerry (End of newsletter quotes and re-publication).

------- ✧ -------

(PLEASE NOTE: The URL quoted above in my newsletter may not stay up forever! Therefore, here is the full article) Border buddies: A merger between the United States and Canada? Visionary writer starts a 'thought experiment' By Meghan Drake - The Washington Times Sunday, March 23, 2014 If Diane Francis had her way, the

U.S. would share a lot more with its northern neighbor than the Great Lakes, maple syrup and Justin Bieber. The editor-at-large for Toronto's National Post argues that a complete merger of Canada and the United States would create a global colossus, add 13 stars to the American flag, eliminate the border and require just a few amendments to the Constitution. But, Ms. Francis acknowledged on a visit to Washington last week, not everyone up north is thrilled with the idea. "I wanted to attack the Canadian establishment and say, 'Wake up, there is [a merger] underway, let's manage it to our benefit,' and to attack American ignorance about Canada," she said. The "thought experiment," first broached in a book she published late last year, was introduced on the 20th anniversary of the North American Free Trade Agreement as President Obama pushed for much broader trade agreements with the European Union and Asia-Pacific nations. Ms. Francis envisions a full-on economic and political merger in which Canada's provinces would become 13 states in the U.S. Quebec would become a commonwealth like Puerto Rico. "If you politically merged the two, Canadians become the fabric softener for the United States," she said last week at a panel discussion at the Woodrow Wilson Center. In her book, "Merger of the Century: Why Canada and America Should Become One Country," Ms. Francis said both sides of the American bipartisan divide could find things to like from the merger. Republicans could point to enhanced security, energy resources and market benefits. For Democrats, the attraction would be the incorporation of an electorate whose political center is far to the left of the U.S. balance of power. Beyond the politics, she conceded that the question remains whether Canadians would transition into an American culture. For reasons political, historical and demographic, "Canadians are very much tinged with the anti-American attitude, there's no question," she said.

The numbers laid out in her book are tempting for a geopolitical strategist: A U.S.-Canada combination would create an economy that is larger than the European Union's, and larger than those of China, Taiwan, Japan and South Korea combined. The North American colossus would control more oil, water, arable land and resources than any other country, all protected by the world's most powerful military. The rest of the world would be fighting for second place in the medal race at the Winter Olympics. While seemingly far-fetched as a political proposition, the merger is already underway with Canadians "voting with their feet," the author argued. Three million Canadians live full or part time in the U.S. During the 20th century, 7 million Canadians immigrated to the United States. An economic merger is much more in reach, particularly with reforms of NAFTA and other policy initiatives, analysts say. With an estimated $616 billion in two-way trade in 2012, Canada retains its long-held position as the largest U.S. trading partner. Ms. Francis said an elimination of the border and the prospect of joint efforts to open the Arctic to economic development suggest an even brighter future. Kevin Lees, founder and editor of the foreign policy journal Suffragio, said the United States can benefit easily and immediately from "low-hanging fruit" in Canada. "The good news is that policymakers on both sides of the border are very much considering those ideas," he said. Chris Wilson, an associate at the Mexico Institute at the Wilson Center, said Canada is the weakest link in the NAFTA pact. "It also has to do with this attitude in Canada that Mexico contaminates its relationship with the United States," he said. "It has to do with this attitude in Canada perhaps even a little bit of jealously about the level of attention that Mexico gets in Washington compared to Canada." Canadian motivation for a political merger may grow as the United States seeks to expand its free trade market by negotiating with the European Union and a group of Pacific Rim nations. "Canada stands to lose an awful lot of trade with the United States, and that will be displaced by sort of trans-Atlantic trade between the United States and the European Union," Mr. Lees said. The United States and Canada may not be merging soon, Ms. Francis acknowledged, but it may happen sooner than many skeptics think. Her book, she noted, talks of the "merger of the century."

She noted, "We have a lot more years in this century."

(End article)

It is a play for oil, of that there is no question. We must also keep in mind that there is something else which I alluded briefly to above and that is fresh water. This SO important that I wish, again, to re-emphasize it. The US is running into problems here with their insistence that their domestic supply will never run dry and that rich builders can become ever richer by raising new cities in desert areas such as Arizona and Nevada. Great golf courses are being constructed as well and there never seems to be a concern as to how the populations here will ever be able to obtain the ever growing supplies of water to make this all work. Even the recent headlines about California looking at poor levels in reservoirs and a possible 500 year drought have not dissuaded the profit-crazed developers. In fact, recently I saw a projection that California by the year 2030 might be looking at a population of perhaps 40 million people. This is considerably more than the entire population of Canada today! It is the incessant desire to grow and build at all costs (and with the possible arrival of millions of new immigrants, this is probably preordained) with no thought as to how to make it work which irritates me. So, the people with the say-so in the United States will be looking at Albertan oil to be sure, but also the immense reserves of fresh water to be found in the Northwest Territories and Nunavut. It is probably the water which will tip the scales when all is said and done. Canada has about 20% of the world's fresh water reserves, more than any other country. It is a prize worth coveting in other words! Given global growth, and shortages in North America this is where the deal for "The Merger" will probably go through. Finally, let me look at another trial balloon being floated here regarding "The Merger". A major Canadian business paper has climbed on board this particular bandwagon in recent months and feels that when all of the assets of a united US/Canada were taken into consideration, every Canadian would be entitled to a lump sum payment of about $US 500,000. Basing this on a German model for their reunification in 1990, it would probably be calculated on years of residency and the actual payout would be factored in over at least two decades. If one thinks about it, if you were given $ 500,000 in one lump sum, what would you do? Well all that nasty credit card debt would be gone in a flash and maybe a nice new house?? Well, what would happen to the price of those houses with everyone trying to buy at the same time? What would happen to the price of cars or the price of anything else for that matter? The West German payout to the old East Germany was well absorbed and there is no reason (according to this article) why a payment to Canadians could not be managed in a similar manner. Lots in this chapter to be sure for you to assess and analyses. What about other ways that Americans could stick their claws into the parts of Canada which really matter? (You can tell where I stand on this issue, can't you??). Well, there is another major possibility and we shall discuss this in our next chapter

SEGMENT THREE

CHAPTER ONE

COLD FUSION – ROOM TEMPERATURE NUKES WITHOUT THE RISK?

Well, now that I have a decent fill (although I could go on for quite a while on that sorry subject!) on nuclear power, let me try something else. One of the things which has always interested me was Cold Fusion. This came out in 1989 and was discovered by Messrs., Pons and Fleishmann of the United States. What is this anyhow?

Well, look at the sun – yep, the one in the sky. It is essentially a ball of gas which has a core temperature of millions of degrees. This does all sorts of things with its atoms of hydrogen gas and effectively squeezes out a lot of energy which heats our Earth and makes it liveable. It is a complex task which our sun does (we still have not yet figured it out and duplicated it well enough to generate the electric power we need) and the above gentlemen wondered if this couldn't be accomplished somehow at room temperature. In other words, instead of the "hot fusion" that we have on the sun, perhaps we could have "cold fusion" which would generate terrific amounts of energy at room temperature.

In 1989, they announced that this had been done and instead of being feted and given every Nobel Prize one can think off, they were excoriated! Almost immediately all sorts of learned scientists (one presumes those who had made their living from "hot fusion" studies) were besides themselves with rage. They claimed that Pons and Fleishmann had not done enough back-up research to be able to publish their works and as such their entire idea of "cold fusion" was null, void, and absolutely without foundation. I wondered about all of this. Were Pons and Fleishmann doing some sort of hush-hush (to use a word often used with "conspiracy theory" type of analysis) research which was to be sent to their principals for private use? While I have not seen any US comments based on this idea over the intervening thirty odd years, I do not see why it cannot be correct. If proven, it would be worth a fortune beyond measure. Imagine, if you will, a brand new method of fueling electricity demand throughout the globe which puts all of the older methods (including nuclear power) out of business. What a gift to mankind! What a benefit! However, cold fusion seems not to have been used to help mankind. (LOTS of vested interests here I would imagine, who would like nothing better than to keep the decaying status quo operational for as long as possible!).

However, not all research is done in the US as there are many other countries with very pressing power needs. Let us consider Japan. This small island nation (less than half the size of Alberta with a population of more than thirty times greater) has few natural resources. They have to import all of their petroleum needs and for them nuclear power (or anything else come to think of it) is of critical importance. So, if they see something like cold fusion they are going to jump all over it. This they did and set up all sorts of research labs to see if they could use what Pons and Fleishmann had apparently discovered. I followed this for several years and saw all sorts of results. Some Japanese labs duplicated the results of the Americans, and others had no luck whatsoever. Still others had mixed results which they were unable to reproduce at all! The Russians were interested but the net effect of all of this is that there does not seem to be a consensus on what Pons and Fleishmann were able to accomplish. What troubles me is that all of the nearly frenzied lab work done on their experiments suddenly came to a halt shortly after the turn of the century and nothing further has been announced. There are two possibilities here. Either there is nothing left to research and Pons and Fleishmann have been proven to be frauds, or else this HAS been proven to work and is being held off the markets for reasons of the immense profit potential. (Politicians being slippery here??).

I think personally, after reviewing all of the material I can find on cold fusion, that it is a valid possibility. If it IS being held back because of profit concerns and so forth, then mankind deserves just about everything which is probably going to happen to him – probably in not that long a period of time.

However, while we should file cold fusion away for future reference as it will almost certainly be brought to the surface again, there are other things to be trotted out. I would now like to examine what is called, somewhat grandly: Solar Power. This is, not surprisingly, energy derived from the sun which is not likely to go out for a VERY long time (several billion years at current estimates). This sounds almost too good to be true, doesn't it?

SEGMENT THREE

OIL AND ALTERNATIVE ENERGY – SLIPPERY
SUBSTANCE VERSUS SLIPPERY POLITICIANS!

CHAPTER TWO

✦ ◆ ✦ ◆ ✦

NUKES – ARE WE REALLY STUCK
WITH THIS MONSTER?

O K, so much for some fun on a subject which is about as serious as one can get. Personally, I do not believe that the leaders of the industrialized world (the politicians I have just referred to, in the final analysis) have any clue as to what they want to do inasmuch as a longer term strategy is concerned. It seems all to be "now, next year, and beyond that – who can tell?" type of arrangement. What clueless leaders don't know, the lap-dog press (sorry to say that, but the quality of investigative journalism seems to be a lot lower than what it was when I was a boy) doesn't really care to comment about in any degree of depth. So, when we are talking about oil and its probable depletion (I refer you back to the comments in a previous chapter under the price phenomenon of "backwardation"), this is but one small element of the overall energy equation. If you have been studying all about this from the press, you will probably have the idea that "if we can't use oil, then wind and solar are the way to go". After propounding your theories to any audience you may have, your idea will probably have firmed into something resembling granite in your mind in that this is what has to be done and what can only be done. There is no other possibility you will say, and you would be quite wrong!

I would ask you to look at nuclear power. Yes, I know that after Fukushima and what could be a horror beyond imagining evolving in the Pacific Ocean, you probably don't want to look at this possibility. Such an energy source is used all over the world, although reactors are quite expensive if all of the safety protocols are adhered to. The nuclear lobby in the United States is a strong one and, to be frank given the very weak leadership in the US Congress, it does not look like anything substantial will happen to this form of generating electric power to any great extent for sometime to come. Of course, if there is another Three Mile Island which is not caught in time, who can tell? France uses this form of electrical generation for about 70% of its power and that REALLY cannot be changed to any great extent very quickly at all without really massive dislocation for the French economy. Well, OK you don't like nukes and to be frank neither do I! I have always looked on nuclear power as something that "if something goes very wrong, are we going to be looking at an event such as Chernobyl, in the modern state of Ukraine, when the area around that city will be uninhabitable for possibly 20,000 years"?

If we go back in time for 20,000 years we are looking at, in general, a caveman/mud-hut type existence. That is a long time. What happens in the 22,000 AD? Is man still around then to wonder about the incredible risks which were taken for short term profits in a period when mankind went, effectively, mad? I have always looked at an analogy here which I would like to share with you. If you are driving in a car and have an accident you may be injured, but you will, in general, be up and about at some future date to resume your life. A crash in a car need not be fatal. If you like flying and have an accident/crash here you have probably had it. You are dead, and all it took was just one accident. If we use this idea for nuclear power we can say that "just one accident" can have unimaginably disastrous effects. There is no picking up the pieces and saying that all will now be fine for us in just a few weeks or months. This is the risk with nuclear power. When it works it works very well indeed and supplies enormous amounts of electric power for cheap domestic consumption and corporate/industrial demand. When it goes wrong, the knock on effects can be dangerous and life-threatening beyond measure. Is this really worth the risk? Can we match off fifty or one hundred years of problem-free generation and easy living against (in the case of Chernobyl) 20,000 years of death and horror beyond imagination? I do not believe we can, although there are plenty of people who are willing to take the other side of this argument. As a former trader (in FX and commodities), I would say that the risk/reward strategy in using nukes are simply not acceptable.

In the German newspapers of May 19, 2014, there was a lively debate about how nuclear plants were to be disassembled in that country and how all this was going to be paid for. This is something that REALLY gets my goat and I want simply write down what I feel and why, and let my (so far) long suffering reader judge for him/herself.

Germany, quite rightly after the disaster which is ongoing at Fukushima (and probably getting much worse, but let's not go into that now), said that they were going to close down their nuclear system and decommission the nuclear power plants. Calling on the great German power companies to do this, Chancellor Merkel started to run into trouble: lots of it. In the beginning when Germany decided to get on board the nuclear power idea, they made the decision that they had to do this because a growing Germany was not going to be able to generate the electric power which it required in any other manner. OK, this makes sense (given what they knew about nuclear dangers at the time) but then they started to go badly wrong. In true post-war capitalistic fashion, they asked the German power generators to step up to the plate and find an efficient method of doing what had to be done. In an equally measured fashion these companies simply said that "the risks were too high and too expensive" and that "the German Government would have to provide funding and lots of it to mitigate the risk".

This the federal German government did and when all of the plants were built the companies started to put the energy out to consumers, and pocketed the money as "profits for taking the risks we did". True, the plants were well run and there were no versions of a German Chernobyl (imagine that in a physically small country like Germany!) but private industry just soaked up the money as it came to them. Yes, they had to contribute to a fund which would be used to retire plants once they had reached the end of their useful lives, and today this comes to about EUR 30 billion. (It seems a lot, but read on). Decade in and decade out shareholders grew fat and rich on all of this until Chancellor Merkel (Germany's leader) decided to shut them down. The companies were not happy with this at all and in the German press in the last few days we are seeing complaints to the effects that "We can't do this ourselves. It is too expensive and the risks are too great". This is virtually the language when they set up the plants several decades ago! What is with these big companies anyhow? They are great at cherry picking it seems and are very happy to get lucrative deals for their shareholders and to tell everyone how well "The System" works, but when things go bad, they run. I suspect that they are seeing (from the benefit of being nuclear insiders) just how bad things are at Fukushima, and how hopelessly overmatched the Japanese company TEPCO is. They want no part of anything even remotely like that happening in Germany.

So, this is how the western economic system works when the chips are down? This is the system which promises so much and what was held up as some sort of incredible economic construct when its main competitor, the Soviet Union, failed? To set up nuclear plants took huge government support.

To de-construct them will apparently take as much or possibly even more which will also require the German Federal Purse to pick up a LOT of the financial bits and pieces. And then there is the question of nuclear waste. What have the German power companies been doing as nuclear fuel has been expended and had to be replaced? It turns out that both the corporations and the government have done precisely nothing! The nuclear poisons were, it seems, to be "someone else's problem". Not anymore is what we can now write here! This will cost enormous amounts of money to resolve (if it can be resolved at all) and that is, of course, "too expensive and too full of risk" for the wretched German companies, who have unlimited access to bank credit of all types no less!

German corporations are tucking their tails between their

collective legs and sulking off a stage which they should never have been on in the first place! I wonder what the Germans, running from a relatively well managed system, can tell us about the Japanese at Fukushima? There the Japanese have their concept of "face" to hide behind, but if one examines how human beings when stressed with this subject react as is the case today, there is apparently much for the inquisitive observer (yours truly!) to learn!

SEGMENT THREE

CHAPTER THREE

COLD FUSION – ROOM TEMPERATURE
NUKES WITHOUT THE RISK?

W

ell, now that I have a decent fill (although I could go on for quite a while on that sorry subject!) on nuclear power, let me try something else. One of the things which has always interested me was Cold Fusion. This came out in 1989 and was discovered by Messrs., Pons and Fleishmann of the United States. What is this anyhow?

Well, look at the sun – yep, the one in the sky. It is essentially a ball of gas which has a core temperature of millions of degrees. This does all sorts of things with its atoms of hydrogen gas and effectively squeezes out a lot of energy which heats our Earth and makes it liveable. It is a complex task which our sun does (we still have not yet figured it out and duplicated it well enough to generate the electric power we need) and the above gentlemen wondered if this couldn't be accomplished somehow at room temperature. In other words, instead of the "hot fusion" that we have on the sun, perhaps we could have "cold fusion" which would generate terrific amounts of energy at room temperature.

In 1989, they announced that this had been done and instead of being feted and given every Nobel Prize one can think off, they were excoriated! Almost immediately all sorts of learned scientists (one presumes those who had made their living from "hot fusion" studies) were besides themselves with rage. They claimed that Pons and Fleishmann had not done enough back-up research to be able to publish their works and as such their entire idea of "cold fusion" was null, void, and absolutely without foundation. I wondered about all of this. Were Pons and Fleishmann doing some sort of hush-hush (to use a word often used with "conspiracy theory" type of analysis) research which was to be sent to their principals for private use? While I have not seen any US comments based on this idea over the intervening thirty odd years, I do not see why it cannot be correct. If proven, it would be worth a fortune beyond measure. Imagine, if you will, a brand new method of fueling electricity demand throughout the globe which puts all of the older methods (including nuclear power) out of business. What a gift to mankind! What a benefit! However, cold fusion seems not to have been used to help mankind. (LOTS of vested interests here I would imagine, who would like nothing better than to keep the decaying status quo operational for as long as possible!).

However, not all research is done in the US as there are many other countries with very pressing power needs. Let us consider Japan. This small island nation (less than half the size of Alberta with a population of more than thirty times greater) has few natural resources. They have to import all of their petroleum needs and for them nuclear power (or anything else come to think of it) is of critical importance. So, if they see something like cold fusion they are going to jump all over it. This they did and set up all sorts of research labs to see if they could use what Pons and Fleishmann had apparently discovered. I followed this for several years and saw all sorts of results. Some Japanese labs duplicated the results of the Americans, and others had no luck whatsoever. Still others had mixed results which they were unable to reproduce at all! The Russians were interested but the net effect of all of this is that there does not seem to be a consensus on what Pons and Fleishmann were able to accomplish. What troubles me is that all of the nearly frenzied lab work done on their experiments suddenly came to a halt shortly after the turn of the century and nothing further has been announced. There are two possibilities here. Either there is nothing left to research and Pons and Fleishmann have been proven to be frauds, or else this HAS been proven to work and is being held off the markets for reasons of the immense profit potential. (Politicians being slippery here??).

I think personally, after reviewing all of the material I can find on cold fusion, that it is a valid possibility. If it IS being held back because of profit concerns and so forth, then mankind deserves just about everything which is probably going to happen to him – probably in not that long a period of time.

However, while we should file cold fusion away for future reference as it will almost certainly be brought to the surface again, there are other things to be trotted out. I would now like to examine what is called, somewhat grandly: Solar Power. This is, not surprisingly, energy derived from the sun which is not likely to go out for a VERY long time (several billion years at current estimates). This sounds almost too good to be true, doesn't it?

SEGMENT THREE

CHAPTER FOUR

+ ◆ ◆ ◆ ◆ ◆ +

SOLAR POWER, SOMETHING WE
CAN ALL UNDERSTAND? NOPE!

However, this understanding I referred to at the end of the last chapter may not be the case. I watched, for many years, a huge EU (European Union) project in the Sahara Desert in Africa. This was designed to get this most inhospitable piece of land to bloom "with a thousand points of light" – well, sort of. You probably know this expression of former President George Bush, but it should probably interpret to get the Sahara to bloom with "a thousand solar collectors".

With all of the sunlight which falls on this massive desert, this sort of Solar Power generator should have been a no-brainer. Nope! You got that one wrong! Has a look at what I wrote in my newsletter not that long ago about this: -

"Do you remember the great initiative by the EU some years back called 'DESERTEC'? It was an attempt to effectively set up a series of solar collectors from across the Sahara and transfer the resulting energy back to the European power grids through Italy. It was an immense project, but the (then) Green EU decided that it was all worth it and they trumpeted the immense benefits at every chance they got. "Politicians lined up to be interviewed and the costs, we were assured, were not that serious when one considered the never ending supply of electricity which would be generated. After all, when does the Sahara Desert become cloudy?? Plans went ahead with the usual gusto until ... one day it all stopped. Politicians were suddenly "too busy" to answer questions about all of this and interest waned with an almost indecent haste. "The idea put out was that with all of the potential civil wars in North Africa, the whole project was just too risky. That was all that was (if I remember correctly) said although there was some talk that technologically speaking the project wouldn't work, and the matter dropped out of sight".

A mess to be sure, but the math, despite all of the official blather from greasy/slippery politicians simply didn't work. It then turned out that the science was not really all that good either! To generate Solar Power, there has to be certain return for shareholders (assuming we stick with the wretched system where "the free market" tells us what wonderful things can be done, but doesn't really deliver all that often). We also have to be aware that to deliver the end product to markets means that it has to be cheaper than other effective sources. This would include the wretched nuclear power, which has never been what was promised in the beginning of its hey-day.

Oil, as it has been plentiful for over a century now (we, in Alberta, are celebrating the first oil wells drilled here a hundred years ago this year), has been something which will "always be there" even though it is patently clear that this can never be. Oil is cheap relative to many other possible energy sources, and certainly so when compared to Solar Power. Therefore, why make the sun work for its keep, when we can just use oil? Yes, it is true that in the beginning of a new technology it will frequently cost a great deal more, but that is before all sorts of new refinements are found and developed which will make the new technology (remember this is solar we are talking about here) cheaper. What happens when it is revealed that Solar Power does not work, and CANNOT work??

In what has to have been a really terrific slap-in-the-face to proponents of this form of "renewable energy", the EU (as can be seen from my newsletter clipping above) simply decided that it didn't work and couldn't work. One day the EU's brain trust (word very loosely used!) decided to re-check the figures from the energy nirvana which was supposed to be DESERTEC. They found, to their horror, that the electricity being claimed from the Sahara would barely light a series of homes and lighthouses in Sicily – just across a narrow portion of the Mediterranean Sea from Africa!! It seems that the technical skills required to send all of this power north to the EU's industrial powerhouse, Germany, simply wasn't there! It had been assumed that this would exist, and that seems to have been a rather poor assumption.

I follow a US equity called "First Solar" or FSLR which is what it trades under on the NASDAQ exchange. For several years after its inception, this traded very nicely under the assumption that "Solar Power" was here to stay and was the wave of the future. The euphoria that the transition from an oil based economy was not based on the reality of the nuts-and-bolts world simply was not seriously considered. The Free Market with all of its mysterious and little understood theories of market efficiencies was simply assumed to be able to provide whatever solutions were required.

When it became clear (ably and assisted by the rumored bankruptcy of a low cost solar panel maker in China) that the entire idea of solar power was simply a chimera, the stock crashed from something like 170 to about 10. This is quite a fall! As I write these words in the Spring of 2014 it has recovered to about 70 or so, which is a decent enough bounce, but is it anything more than this? After all, if a low cost producer in China cannot make the producers cheap enough for solar panels for western economies and the technology is suspect at best, what is the purpose of Solar Power even existing; much less FSLR and its competitors? I addressed this in my newsletters over the DESERTEC commentary above.

What is immediately below is also a decent commentary to what is probably official EU thinking as well. I think that what I wrote then, is quite good enough for now, and I shall prove this (hopefully to your satisfaction!) to a greater extent in the forthcoming paragraphs. Here is another brief newsletter clipping:-

"The US and the EU have lots of money and credit to take a major flyer on something like DESERTEC if either so chose. The money, through official channels in one form or another, is simply not forthcoming now and I wonder if the stock market got wind of this and this is the reason why First Solar was driven through the floor two years ago? "If the money (as with wind power) is not available for something which is so critical for the EU, then something is seriously wrong somewhere: to be admitted or not. The EU, to come full circle with this set of essays, knows a very great deal about what is happening with various forms of power generation and has decided (being nice and quiet in true bureaucratic fashion) that there is very little alternative (if any) to simple, good old fashioned oil. "This is true in a traditional sense from experience over the last century or so, and so we go down the Fracking trail which, if many US oil engineers are to be listened to, is only a temporary palliative at best. What is the EU going to do, now that they have effectively said that they are bankrupt of new ideas and can only, feebly, embrace technologies which they have scorned quite openly – at least until a few months ago? "Needless to say, this is all very bad news for Europe!"

OK, so what did the EU do then? Well, it seems to have taken a page out of the modern US book for oil drilling and has endorsed fracking (!!). Nothing less than two exclamation points for this one as the EU is supposedly one of the greenest entities on the face of the planet, and fracking (usually considered "dirty oil") is what the Germans might refer to as verboten! Here is an interesting essay from the leading German newspaper der Spiegel on this: (I really do suggest you read this in full at http://www.spiegel.de/international/europe/european-commission-move-away-from-climate-protection-goals-a-943664.html) "Green Fade-Out: Europe to Ditch Climate Protection Goals By Gregor Peter Schmitz in Brussels DPA Europe may be backing away from its ambitious climate protection goals. The EU's reputation as a model of environmental responsibility may soon be history. The European Commission wants to forgo ambitious climate protection goals and pave the way for fracking -- jeopardizing Germany's touted energy revolution in the process. The climate between Brussels and Berlin is polluted, something European Commission officials attribute, among other things, to the "reckless" way German Chancellor Angela Merkel blocked stricter exhaust emissions during her re-election campaign to placate domestic automotive manufacturers like Daimler and BMW. This kind of blatant self-interest, officials complained at the time, is poisoning the climate. But now it seems that the climate is no longer of much importance to the European Commission, the EU's executive branch, either. Commission sources have long been hinting that the body intends to move away from ambitious climate protection goals. On Tuesday, the Süddeutsche Zeitung reported as much. At the request of Commission President José Manuel Barroso, EU member states are no longer to receive specific guidelines for the development of renewable energy. The stated aim of increasing the share of green energy across the EU to up to 27 percent will hold. But how seriously countries tackle this project will no longer be regulated within the plan. As of 2020 at the latest -- when the current commitment to further increase the share of green energy expires -- climate protection in the EU will apparently be pursued on a voluntary basis.

Climate Leaders No More? With such a policy, the European Union is seriously jeopardizing its global climate leadership role. Back in 2007, when Germany held the European Council presidency, the body decided on a climate and energy legislation package known as the "20-20-20" targets, to be fulfilled by the year 2020. They included:

- a 20 percent reduction in EU greenhouse gas emissions;
- raising the share of EU energy consumption produced from renewable resources to 20 percent;
- and a 20 percent improvement in the EU's energy efficiency. All of the goals were formulated relative to 1990 levels. And the targets could very well be met. But in the future, European climate and energy policy may be limited to just a single project: reducing greenhouse gas emissions. The Commission plans also set no new binding rules for energy efficiency". <snip> Well, when the EU comes full

circle on this they REALLY don't play around! Interestingly enough, I didn't see any follow on articles about this in the German press (which I personally regard as among the most environmentally conscientious in the EU). It also says a great deal. Oil is going to be in our future for a long time to come (no matter how the art of fracking manages to hold up – it is a short run phenomenon at best) and the "best minds" in the EU have come to this conclusion and that is apparently that!

So, the EU has effectively thrown in the towel on climate change and given the level of brain power in Brussels, I suspect that there may be something else in play. I shall return to this a bit later on, but before we leave (for the time being) our commentaries on Solar Power I should look at what the UN has been talking about on this. One would have thought that on such an important subject as essentially saving the world from man made climate changes (if this is, as Al Gore suggests, correct) people from around our planet would be talking to each other on an ongoing basis. This does not seem to be so. As has been the case with so many major possibilities in history, the world is divided into major power blocs each with its own agenda for dominating a particular theme.

How is this so? Well, we have just had a good look at how the European power bloc (as represented by the EU) feels about fracking and how they have changed their minds completely on what this represents to the future of Europe. What about the UN? To be frank, I have never been a fan of the United Nations. It is a cess pit of political intrigue where it disproves its founding principles daily of mankind working together. I remember well in the Reagan Administration when, at a press conference, someone pointed out that the UN had condemned something which the Administration had done. In any event, it had incurred the wrath of the White House and in a press conference the speaker merely told the reporter who had brought up the question that (effectively) "Who cares what a debating society two hundred miles from here thinks"? The speaker was never disciplined for these supposedly intemperate remarks which can only lead one to assume that he spoke as he did with the full backing of the powers-that-be (powers that were?) in Washington.

Today, whenever Washington wants something done it is always "The will of the international community" when this is approved. When something is NOT done it is "XXX country has once again flaunted the will of the international community" – as if there is any such thing in reality.

So given that the major world powers apparently feel little more than contempt for the UN and what it apparently stands for, is it any wonder that little in the way of communication is accomplished between New York and, say, the EU? Again, in my view, the sooner this joke of a debating society is wound up the better off we shall be. OK, now that I have got that off my chest, I can make the simple comment that is it any wonder the UN comes out with a long term energy plan which apparently runs completely counter to what the EU has had to say in at least a portion of its report? The noted British newspaper, The Telegraph, came out with a very good story not that long ago about how we are all going to have to adopt renewables as our main source of energy in the balance of this century. Have a look:-

UN green police say ditch oil and change your diet A report by the UN's Intergovernmental Panel on Climate Change calls for "large-scale changes in the global energy system" By Robert Mendick, Chief Reporter 9:00PM BST 12 Apr 2014 Governments must switch from fossil fuels to nuclear, wind and solar energy to avoid a global-warming catastrophe in a move costing about £300 billion a year, a United Nations report warns. The study, by the UN's Intergovernmental Panel on Climate Change (IPCC), lays out the pressing need for the world to ditch coal and oil and switch to green energy. However, the report is likely to spark a new row over the cost of countering global warming. Climate-change sceptics issued a warning to governments not to succumb to a green agenda, alleging that to do so would drive up living costs for the rest of the century. A leaked draft of the report, obtained by The Telegraph, provides a blueprint on how to tackle climate change, including not only the switch to green energy but even what people should eat. It claims: Þ An estimated £300 billion a year is needed for investment in low-carbon sources of electricity such as nuclear, wind and solar energy over the next 20 years; Þ Gas should replace coal-fired power stations as soon as possible to reduce carbon emissions, although gas should eventually be phased out, too; Þ Nuclear power is an established method for producing low-carbon electricity, although the report notes its use has waned since 1993; Þ Experts estimate that by 2030, global gross domestic product (GDP) could be as much as 4 per cent lower through measures to combat global warming. By 2100, global GDP could be down by as much as 12 per cent; Þ Western diets need to become more sustainable and environmentally friendly. This is likely to include a call to eat less meat. The change of lifestyle is not mapped out in detail but the UN suggests that people living in the richest countries should eat less. That advice will inevitably lead to accusations that the UN is interfering in personal habits. The central thrust of the report will be a call for "large-scale changes in the global energy system" and increased subsidy for green energy to help countries make the switch from fossil fuels. The cost of doing so, according to the 29-page draft summary, will require an additional £90 billion a year investment, a rise of a third on estimates of current spending. That will take the total investment in low carbon energy sources to about £300 billion a year until 2030. Britain now spends about £6 billion a year, trying to cut greenhouse gas emissions through such measures as subsidies for wind farms and solar power. There will be pressure for that figure to rise sharply. The report warns that to achieve a target of keeping the global temperature rise to within 3.6F (2C) by the end of the century will require spending on alternative energy and a scaling back of fossil fuels that, the report acknowledges, will damage economic growth. The call for a change in energy policy will inevitably lead to further tensions in the Coalition with many back-bench Conservatives anxious that wind power is too expensive and the turbines unsightly. Many Tories are pushing for the exploitation of underground shale gas reserves through the controversial process of fracking to extract the gas. Fracking has become big business in the US and driven down the cost of energy. Ed Davey, the Liberal Democrat Energy and Climate Change Secretary, is likely to seize upon the report to resist further demands to cut green energy subsidies. Senior Tory MPs warned the Government not to succumb to pressure from the UN to plough more money into renewable energy, driving up household energy bills and threatening to make British industry uncompetitive in the process. Chris Heaton-Harris, a Conservative MP who led a successful back-bench campaign to cut the consumer subsidy to wind farms, said: "This IPCC report is backward looking. We can be a lot greener, emit less carbon and produce cheaper energy if we switch to shale gas rather than ploughing our money into wind farms that plunge the poorest people into fuel poverty." Benny Peiser, director of the Global Warming Policy Foundation, a think tank that has warned against the cost of switching to green energy, said: "Even if the IPCC assumptions prove correct, it will be much more cost effective and rational to invest in adaptation strategies to deal with climate change than try to decarbonise the world economy." However, Bob Ward, policy director of the Grantham Research Institute on Climate Change, based at the London School of Economics, said: "This report shows that if we carry on the way we are going, it will be much more expensive and risky to take action later on." The IPCC report into man-made climate change is the most authoritative of its kind and forms the basis for policymaking among UN member nations. Last week, government officials meeting in Berlin were combing through the draft report to come up with a final document countries can agree upon. World leaders will gather at a specially convened UN conference in New York in September, before approving a new set of international agreements on carbon emissions in Paris next year. The new report will form the basis for those negotiations. Here is the URL: http://www.telegraph.co.uk/earth/environment/climatechange/10763080/UN-green-police-say-ditch-oil-and-change-your-diet.html"

In reviewing this brief story, one is struck with the concept that the "big brains" at the various UN agencies – this outfit just grows and grows bureaucratically, with YOU paying for it – have come to the conclusion that we have to de-carbonise the world and to adopt renewables. We are also seeing something which I do not like, and that is the fact that we shall all have to change our diets. This means, in all probability, that we westerners are going to have to get along with less red meat as there may be less grain to feed the cattle which much of our diet come from in the main. This belief seems rooted in the consciousness of UN planners, despite the fact that cattle are much tastier when reared on grass. Just turn them loose on the open prairie and you will have better cattle with better meat (with, the obvious corollary being that there will be a LOT of grain freed up for other more pressing needs). However, grain and some sort of growing political belief that it is somehow "wrong" to eat poor, defenseless cattle, is going to become a growing UN-inspired problem as we move forward. Let us return to the de-carbonised world. I have studied this for many years/decades and I simply cannot agree with what they are saying. The basic idea of the UN think tanks is that the atmosphere of the world is being heavily polluted by the mass burning and consumption of hydrocarbons and such will have to be radically curtailed. Many US right-wingers feel that what the UN would really like to do is to push mankind (read Americans) into larger and larger cities with very limited mobility. The idea is that with a large chunk of Americans in such living conditions, most of the rest will be left on existing farms to provide food for the cities and to grow such food under very strict protocols. The rest of the country would be given back to Nature to allow "Mother Earth" to heal herself from the raping it has endured under man's tutelage for so many centuries now.

What strikes me is that this "Agenda-21" (as it has come to be called after its presentation in Rio de Janerio (Brazil) in 1992) is assumed to be the only solution for what are, admittedly, very real problems on the face of an increasingly exhausted planet. All of this planning is quite remarkable for what is little more than a global debating society! There are, of course, many other solutions to what we have to face up to in the coming decades and we shall examine these as this book progresses.

As I was saying above, the UN seems to regard itself as some sort of unerring institution and its dictates are to be obeyed as they are the product of the "very finest minds" the planet has to offer. I am sure that the EU would not agree with this at all! The big thing to note here is that the EU thinkers tend to regard what has to be done from a more practical bent. They have all been quite happy with the concept of Solar Power until they were apparently convinced that their desires (planned society?) were not achievable. They changed (as we have discovered) to adopting the idea of frackable oil and Natural Gas (possibly inspired by a possible Russian boycott of the EU if things got nasty with the Ukraine, which they clearly have). How long will they continue with this (for them) unusual tactic?

With the EU's economy in close to ruins, as the EU is starting to find out that not all countries can use a currency (the Euro) which is suitable for Germany and few others, they cannot afford further declines. However, this means little to the UN it seems. There we have a mandate, as The Telegraph article strongly implies, that renewables will be the way to go. Oblivious to the fact that the science may not work at all, the implied comment from the UN is that "we have to make it work". This is an audacious and frankly arrogant approach for the debating society to adopt for the world! Well, let us finish off the comments on Solar Power by returning to our friend "FSLR" (or First Solar). We have noted that its price soared into the financial stratosphere when it started operations on wild optimism that Solar Power would be a large portion of what was needed to save mankind from being cooked to death by global warming and our insane desire to burn as much fossil fuel as possible for generally minor things – such as long distance driving on vacations and the like.

We could also note here that another so called frivolous item would be the practice of growing iceberg lettuce in California and the trucking of it 3,000 miles to markets in Maine. However, that is an Agenda 21 worry – not ours – so let us return to what FSLR's stock price might be telling us. We have seen that it went from an absurd overvaluation in the 160/170 range all the way down to 10 or so briefly. Then what happened? As is usual with this sort of price collapse, there were the generally dismal stories that FSLR didn't have the cash to keep going and that it would not be able to sell solar panels because of severe price undercutting from China. Then the Chinese firm went bankrupt because "it couldn't make a go of solar" and on and on it went. These things are typical of a market bottom where any and all rumours, no matter how wild, are deemed to be newsworthy. However, someone did start buying down there (an insider who couldn't believe the bargain FSLR at represented? – it happens), and we started to rebound slowly. Today (May 12, 2014) it looks quite good at near 70. If you are a technical analysis person (or at least sympathetic to the concept) we can say that it has now retraced all of the losses to this level which happens to be the 200 week Simple Moving Average. Technical theory now holds that if we can break this to the upside on a weekly close and then open higher the next week, we probably have a good intermediate term buying signal. Of interest, we did try for week after week some months ago to break through this major moving average and it looks like we have failed as the market has come back lower to the 58 area. (This is before it bounced back to close through the 70 barrier). By the way, while I have your attention please do not say something like "Moving Averages? They are just wiggly lines on a bit of paper which mean nothing at all". I took my first lesson in "wiggly lines" back in 1962 when this science was popular, in general, in certain areas of the dealing community. They are STILL popular and if they had no significance, this would not be the case among cash-starved and profit hungry dealers. Anyway, to finish off my story on FSLR, let me say that we can still break the 70 line (although perhaps not immediately) and when that happens we shall see buyers of all descriptions pile in to buy "because the technical signal has been broken and if I don't buy someone else will". True enough I guess, but what does this say about buying a security on the basis of "the fundamentals are good and are likely to be so for a long time to come"? In other words, it doesn't matter if Solar Power is a viable idea or not! People will buy because others are buying (again, so much for independent thought and analysis!) and the rumour will be "the insiders are buying and if it is good enough for them then it is good enough for me!". To put all of this yet another way, this stock can go to the moon because "it is the wave of the future". It makes no difference if the future leaves this technology in the dust, its stocks will be bought anyhow! Read the bit about the UN which I wrote earlier on. The UN says that it must work and accordingly it will be made to work. (Hey ... if it is good enough for the world's premier debating society ...).

Well, let's bring an end to Solar Power, at least for now. It seems clear to me that with so many really well-to-do types who apparently believe in Solar Power, that something will be found to support this concept and bring it to the attention of the ever gullible public.

Any losses, as so often happens, will probably be lumped onto these poor souls via the mechanism of a collapsing share price. The profits (assuming that the technical difficulties can be overcome and some sort of viable system comes to the fore to rescue The Debating Society – henceforth capitalised!) will go to where profits usually go I suspect ('nuff said?!). Just remember the lessons of DESERTEC! If a power starved society such as the EU cannot make a go of Solar Power in an area of the world which is about as solar friendly as it is possible to get (the Sahara Desert), it is going to take a GREAT breakthrough to make all of this finally work at all!

SEGMENT FOUR

CHAPTER ONE

———————— ◆◆◆◆◆◆ ————————

THE CASHLESS SOCIETY (AHHH ... WHO NEEDS PAPER MONEY ANYWAY?)

Yeah ... a society where computers dominate and we do not have the "filthy lucre" (aka cash money – dollar bills) in our pockets. Sounds good right? Well it does at least until the computer breaks down at the store and you can't buy groceries, or a child's favourite confection when s/he is screaming so loudly that you can barely hear yourself think and other customers are staring daggers at you!

Ah, the joys of modern North American life! At least in this example you can buy your way out of the store with some soiled (but valid) bank notes and these NEVER "go down" or suffer from an unplanned power outage in a savage storm.

Yes, we can make all sorts of comments along these lines, but the fact of the matter is the trend and this is that every few years computer abilities double on a compound basis. The time is surely coming when profit-hungry bankers and desperately cash strapped governments will simply mandate that cash is no longer acceptable as a means of transacting business or (most importantly from their perspective), paying taxes of all sorts.

In my newsletter a few months ago I had a good look at all of this and wish to share with you my thoughts from that time (as they really haven't changed very much, if at all). Yes, I take awhile to seemingly get to the point, but have faith! I do get there and hopefully all will be made clear as I do.

What I am afraid of is that the powers-that-be in Washington have planned for a cashless society for a long time. Without advanced computers, this was impossible as there did not exist the storage technology to get all of hundreds of millions of individual transactions put through to the correct bank accounts in a timely manner. Clearly, if people did not have the faith to transact their business when the end result was anything less than assured, a move to a cashless system would be impossible. However, the miracles wrought by Messrs., Gates, Allen, Jobs et al., have done away with these fears just about completely it seems to me. The grip on the overall economy by the people who wish for this sort of thing to happen has tightened dramatically in just the past decade or so. All right then, without readers jumping up and down screaming "conspiracy nut – why did I waste my money in buying this book?", I must justify what I have been talking about. I hope I can, although I fear that many people will not accept whatever I write. Ok, I honour that, but at least give me the chance to try and get across my point.

There are many people who feel that there is a group of very well-to-do folk who wish to rule over us simply because "it is their right". They go by various names such as Illuminati, Octopus, Bilderbergers, you name it. Wealth begets power (I hope you will grant me that at any rate!) and if you are a multi-billionaire with few areas of the world left to conquer with your wealth in your chosen field, then it is believed (reasonable given human nature I think) that these people will try to go after absolute control over everything.

Wealth is a club and they know how to use it. This sort of behaviour has been known since the days of the prophets in The Old Testament and I quote the Book of Habakkuk Chapter 2, Verse 5 here when he talks about Death (with a capital "D", in other words the Devil) always looking for more and more souls to grab for himself. The relevant passage reads:- "Moreover, wealth is treacherous; the arrogant do not endure. They open their throats wide as Sheol; like Death they never have enough. They gather all nations for themselves, and collect all peoples as their own".

This is a pretty damning indictment, not so much on having wealth but having great financial accumulations and then not using them wisely. The Bible is filled with exhortations about helping the poor, the dispossessed, orphans, and widows, and yet while we do have the odd Bill Gates or Warren Buffett who are doing something with their incredible riches, I suspect that there are many, many others who care only about having "their throats open" and getting more and more no matter what misery they cause in so doing.

With great wealth comes great responsibility, but that is apparently unknown to so many; poor wretches (in the eyes of God) that they are. However we have to realise that over two thousand years ago the prophets in The Bible knew well what human nature would do with great wealth, and they wrote about it at length. Human nature does not change it seems and we must, in looking at how the hidden rich today use their wealth, understand this. If The Bible can give us a lot of lessons about Pi and Fibonacci, then why can it not do something similar in a blunt assessment of human nature?

So, the very well-to-do wish to extend their grasp of the world it seems. But what would they gain with all of this "cashless society talk" if/when it ever comes? All of the talk one sees on this subject tends to fall along the lines of control. Do you recall the controversy last Fall (2013) when JP Morgan/Chase bank was supposed to have placed limits on wires of money/assets leaving the USA? This was not followed up by other banks of any reasonable description and so, under pressure from coin dealers (if no one else), the bank backed down and we returned to the status quo ante when people forgot that this ever happened. Except that it DID happen although not permanently at that time. Was it some sort of trial balloon for use when a truly cashless society comes to pass? If what Chase had talked about ever came to pass on a more global scale across the US banking system (and how would that have affected the use of the US$ as the world's Reserve Currency I wonder?) then any and all securities transactions could have been easily monitored by virtually anybody looking to see what various rich Americans were doing. If somebody wanted to import a large number of silver or gold coins from abroad then this might be of great interest to various agencies wondering about the personal confidence (or lack of same) by some US citizens looking to diversify out of US$, at least to an extent.

As I said, this all came to naught ... at least for now! However as an old friend once told me (who had studied these things throughout his life) "With these people it is always two steps forward and one step back. Once they have come to a decision on what they are going to do, they do not back down or reverse their plans". OK, so if this IS the case, then the move towards cashless transactions will continue to grind inexorably onwards. What is the next step, and given what our Pi Cycle analysis has taught us so far it has to be quite quick. There have been some trial balloons floated, the most notable being that within the next few years people will have to have some sort of chip implanted into their arms so that they may be traced no matter where they go and no matter what they want to purchase and so forth.

When I was made aware of this, I wrote back to the person making these thoughts available and told him about the old ideas from the 1960s and 1970s when many "full blown nut cases" (as they were referred to back then) would advocate wearing a tin-foil hat when they went outside. This would be to avoid either having their mind read by orbiting satellites or to have some sort of ideas implanted by these same satellites. Given how far computer technology has come since the days when these wretched individuals told anybody and everybody about their concerns, maybe they weren't so far away from ultimate reality! The technology may not be able to be devised fast enough to suit the Pi Cycle timeline and at the same time have it accepted in large part by a very dumbed down population. So, given where we are today with credit cards, debit cards, and goodness knows what else, the ultimate rulers of our society (and I am sure they exist as Habakkuk wrote all of these centuries ago) will have to play on existing fears and outright paranoia which does not seem to be that far below the surface these days. What I suspect will happen is that cash will start to be demonised as "being fundamental to the financing of terrorism" or some such. At the same time Gold bullion will also come under increasing attack but, since the days of President Nixon severing the link between the US$ and Gold back in August 1971, this metal has been generally held in very low public esteem by Washington power brokers. The average American, as far as I can see, does not understand how Gold operates as a hedge and would, therefore, probably accept this line of reasoning being given to him/her.

In any event, control of your bank account (not to mention securities accounts) would be a welcome prize to those who seek it. Without cash, and only electronic access to your account, you are vulnerable to hacking and court ordered seizure on what could be rather flimsy evidence. Today, if you feel really threatened, you can withdraw a decent sized amount of cash and spend it as required. Yes, I know all about the official condemnation of large amounts of cash as being de facto evidence of your being a drug smuggler or some sort of tax dodger and I didn't say that living off large amounts of cash would be easy, but it is theoretically doable. This option is completely removed with an electronic form of banking. Look at things this way. Today people are told, relentlessly, that various US security organs can track every word you write/text/email/whatever. There is no privacy left and it seems as though the US court system is not going to stand in the way of this at all. The war against terrorism will not be lost because of some legalistic mumbo-jumbo seems to be the message. Well, if all of this is true with your communications, why is it such a long leap of faith to see that this can also be done with your bank accounts and so forth? It isn't.

So, if we have some sort of false flag event (and this could be a type of illness which, it is claimed, can be traced to "old and diseased banknotes") whereby the US authorities can start to withdraw said forms of paper money, then it will happen. People will be frightened to use cash for fear of "getting sick" and so they won't and will actually demand that cash be severely restricted or even removed from circulation! In fact, come to think of it, I now favour some such illness claim as a way to get banknotes removed! No muss, no fuss!

For those people who live overseas and who use paper money rather extensively, we might even have cell phones act as a form of "no cash banks". Don't laugh! I read (courtesy of the highly respected German daily Der Spiegel) that there are people in Rwanda, East Africa, (of genocide fame from only a few years ago) who are working hard on designing this technology so that people in very remote areas of that country can use their cell phones to buy and sell! It also seems that many African countries have a higher penetration of cell phone usage and possession than the United States itself! If it can be done in Africa, it can be done anywhere is probably the message we can take away from this. In US dominated Europe (culturally if nothing else) it would be a fairly easy sell I would think.

If paper money equals disease with a high probability of death in the USA, why would that logic not hold true in the very federalised EU?? It would hold true, which would mean that in a very short period of time paper money in the West might become passé. Now for my comments in the newsletters of a few months ago. At the end of these, I wish to write a small piece on how this ultimately unfolds. (These newsletter comments are a few paragraphs down).

HINT: Given that this is The End Times and that it involves the US and the US$, we are looking at something truly draconian developing. Go The Book of Revelation again please. Now look at the description of "666". It must be (again, if all my suppositions are correct) the ultimate control mechanism and I have broken this down so you can see how it comes about. It IS based on the name of a man, George Washington (!!). The average person is to be damned, according to The Book of Revelation, for taking this "666" mark willingly and worshipping the issuer of the mark. I do not wish to see scores of millions of Americans condemned in the eyes of God for taking this mark when they haven't a clue as to what it could be and are (most probably being told to believe this) that it is merely a simple way to "take care of your money with the absolute security of the US Government behind it. No muss, no fuss, no terrorism, no drugs, no drug trade, and it is all to make your life a lot simpler". We shall probably be told that a "mark is much easier to handle because, unlike a piece of paper which could be stolen or lost, the mark can never be lost or 'cannot be found' ". Please consider all of this very carefully. I do not claim to be some sort of "all-knowing" person when it comes to this or anything else for that matter. What I am is a long term trader who knows how to follow a trend very well. The cashless society is just such a cultural and societal trend. I am following it. I have come to "666" and wish to warn you as explicitly as I can. Plan your lives as though cashlessness is a done deal and is coming soon. It is. I expect this, using Pi Analysis, for it to be here by 2024/2025 at the latest (ie 2014 War Cycle Year, plus 11 - yep! that number again!). Do not enter into this blindly now! THINK!!! Now for the newsletters which I wrote on this, for your perusal:-

"I have been thinking about this for some time now and while, with the continuing advances in computer science this is going to happen, I have to make sure that I do not seem to be like some sort of frothing-at-the-mouth radical with my views. I do not believe that this is to be the case here, and I shall simply follow the money to see where it leads in the principal circumstance. "The main thing to note here is that the US federal government (as a useful proxy for other 'advanced' governments around the world) is running deficits which are of the most mind-boggling dimensions, seemingly each and every year. The total debt is, as of today's date, November 15, 2013, is a staggering $ 17.1 trillion. "The rate of accumulation of this debt is not going to slow down, in my view, as increasing trends such as this usually have a blow-off of some sort in a short period of time. Marty Armstrong (yep, him again!) is on record as showing us that as of October 2015 the debt becomes so bad that there is a global revulsion for government/sovereign debt, and this is now less than two years away. My own Biblical analysis, presented for your consideration recently, shows almost exactly the same thing. "Reluctantly (as the implications are so bad) I have to agree with Armstrong as I trust I made clear in these recent Biblical analyses. For once, at that time, the US financial nay-sayers who have been wrong for literally decades now, will have their day in the sun. How high will this 'blow off' number finally reach before it all comes tumbling down? "If we have a decent sized war followed by an enhanced economic slowdown, then it is not impossible for us to see a figure of perhaps $ 30 trillion before the general revulsion for these sorts of numbers forces some sort of global buyers strike for US paper (and hence probably other over-indebted nations securities as well).

"So, what has this got to do with a cashless society? Well, it has everything to do with it actually! It has been written in several forums that the US tax gatherers are very concerned that people who deal in cash are not going to report their full and complete incomes, and hence not be charged the proper tax rates. "Over the years there have been many laws passed against people dealing in cash who are made to feel that they are doing something 'dirty and improper' somehow. This 'war on cash' does not seem likely to abate with the large and growing deficits, and the logical conclusion is that ALL cash will have to be withdrawn from circulation at some point, probably in the not too distant future. "One can say that there is to be a fairly severe element of control here. If a society cannot spend as it wishes (collectively) because the powers-that-be do not trust the citizens to be honest and forthright, then we are looking at a society which probably has, at best, a limited future. How is this so? To have a pure cashless society where everything and anything is overseen, means that all is monitored by computers of ever increasing complexity.

"Today, I saw something which made me wonder just how far down this particular path we are going to travel. A new series of algorithms has been discovered in Toronto in which computers can assess "1s" and "0"s and assess them at the same time as opposed to having a choice between the two possibilities. (I am not a computer guru by the way!). "Apparently this boosts computing power by large amounts which, in turn, suggests that it is coming along at just the right time to be the control mechanism for a future cashless society.

(Interesting, isn't it, how these things always seem to come together just when they are needed?). "In extremis, we can say that the Biblical '666' (or '616' if you wish, see below) is the ultimate cashless society code for control over what assets you have and how you spend them. I visited this theme in a recent newsletter on Revelation, and I do not see what is incorrect with it. It follows the money and seems to be a logical extension to where we are going. "If we have a federal database which tracks what every citizen is doing financially, then such a database (presumably run out of Washington DC, as that also seems to be the direction in which we are headed) could be easily modified to prevent anybody who is in not in favour with the federal government from buying or selling anything at all. An average person will have a mark on the right hand or forehead (perhaps even a tattoo for the 'gotta be with it crowd') which might read 'DC 999-99-9999 L' with one's coded Social Security number being the digits.

"It would be machine readable, clearly, and be marketed as something which is a natural outgrowth of the changes in society over the past generation or so, and which would (of course) 'place a crippling burden on the terrorists and drug dealers'. It would be something to 'make us all that much safer' in other words. I believe that this would sell, and sell fairly easily. "Well, what about the drug trade, which I would have thought would be the ultimate cash only trade? Some years ago this was estimated to be something like 5% of the US economy, which would amount to $ 750 billion – $ 1 trillion today. This a gargantuan sum of money and an unbelievable stack of $ 100 bills if indeed drugs are still traded in this manner. "An article in the German daily, Der Spiegel, told of how the drug flow works. It seems to start in the growing fields of Columbia and then makes it way through Panama and Mexico to the US in Texas. It then runs to New York and then to Europe. It pays the growers some EUR 3,000/ kg and the price in the EU runs from EUR 30,000 to EUR 90,000/ kg which is quite a mark-up!

"It is clearly very profitable, although not without risks, and I simply cannot see this being closed down because someone in

Washington gets it in their heads to stop all cash transactions. In other words, in the real world, there are too many important wheels greased with this money for it to be stopped. If it is, then what can be used as a cash substitute? I do not know. Readers, if this cashless society dream/nightmare becomes reality, what do you think? "However, this sort of transaction lies at the periphery of society in the final analysis. If there is to be a major crisis developing in the US (and hence the world because of the liquidity significance of US Treasury securities) then the general weaknesses of the current US financial system will come swiftly to light. "I am referring to the huge US trade imbalance, whereby (it seems to me) that US companies manufacture all sorts of goods in China or other third World nations to be shipped back to the US. It is a short-sighted approach to making the proverbial quick buck and at some point the US$ rate of exchange will have to suffer and suffer badly. This is not yet however.

"The yawning budget deficit is unlikely to be addressed as far as I can see as we are approaching the 'blow off' point noted a day or so ago here. Overall, the Tea Party will probably be proven correct with their fears of a runaway accumulation of US federal debt in my view: for whatever good that will do in a strict economic sense. "The biggest problem will be the private pension funds which are now being crucified with their holdings of US Treasury certificates which yield nearly nothing in returns. I shall be re-examining this issue early in the new year, but my guess at this preliminary stage is that these funds will be nationalised so that 'our older citizens pensions can be made secure and worry free'.

"People who fear a nationalized health care system in the US today are going to be shown to have nothing to worry about here given what can happen with pensions! "The point is that when the well-to-do see the sorts of disasters starting to unfold with Treasuries and the economic infrastructure breaking down, they will want to run with whatever they can take with them – money wise. At that time (as I mentioned in the series of exchange controls which look to be being initiated by Chase bank) this action will probably be too late. "At that time, running with cash money will not be possible as far as I can see as we might be just about cashless overall. In other words, running with a lot of cash to Canada to send money wherever, will not be that viable a proposition. Wiring money to a major centre overseas from home will also be tracked and probably blocked by the Fed or Treasury. You will have left it too late! "If you are going to do anything of a precipitous nature, then take your lesson from investment guru Jim Rogers and his move to a nice apartment in Singapore a year or so ago. With a major US$ crisis (crises) brewing, I can tell you from watching Europe in the 1970s that all of the dollars (in this case) will be blocked from leaving the US, and the benefit thereby to the US economy will be that the US$, which then cannot be sold overseas, will thus be spent/invested in the US. How's that for the stuff which I used to do in my real working life?! (Hint: the US$ exchange rate will not take the pounding it would have were there no exchange controls).

"So, let's try to sum all of this up. I have never liked a cashless society as one always has to worry about going to the grocery store and seeing a sign to the effect 'Sorry, our computers are down'. With cash this cannot, of course, happen. "With US$ cash, one can always take a trip overseas as US$ cash is always welcome because the US$ is the reserve currency of the world (however long that lasts with any distortions which transpire during the transition to a cashless domestic society). This welcome will all be gone and one risks a 'Sorry, cash only, our computers do not accept domestic US cash cards'. Every penny you have will be in a bank (never under the mattress) or a securities or real estate account and therefore at risk of some sort of seizure on any pretext. "You cannot control your own future and the time will come (as noted in a previous essay, I am thinking 2024/25) when a very nasty controlling agency in Washington will simply say that unless you have a 'DC 999-99-9999 L' account marked on your forehead or right hand (when we shall be told that 'this prevents you losing a paper card or having it stolen – it is for your protection') you cannot buy or sell anything which is not approved for you. You will have nothing at all! "Now the only question is how fast this will all play out. My guess is that if you have financial assets you will be amazed at how fast you no longer have any control over a decent portion of them! Be prepared: it is coming!".

End of newsletter quotes. Now let's finish off this chapter by seeing exactly what "666" (OK, or "616") really is and how it is derived in today's modern world.

―――――◆❧◆―――――

What has been written above (for the first three newsletter updates and today) is a fair sized chunk of material to be absorbed, at the very least. There is a lot of conjecture which may be dismissed by the reader as "imaginative" and so forth and I appreciate this divergence of opinion. Fair enough, but there remains just one more idea to place before you which can prove all of this when the time finally comes. How does "666" actually work, if it indeed does refer to Washington DC? Here is my interpretation on what an increasingly authoritarian Washington bureaucracy might try as it struggles to maintain a hold on an increasingly restive, rebellious, population.

Hint: watch for something to happen on "L" Street in DC as we move towards a system where "people cannot buy nor sell without the Mark/Number of The Beast on their right hand or forehead". Have a look and remember "L" street for a new bureaucracy dealing with this sort of (cashless society!) transactions.

Consider this- 1) If "666" refers to tightened financial and cultural control in the US, then Washington DC must be involved. 2) D=500 in Latin numerology; C= 100. So DC = 600. 3) George Washington, the founder of the city which bears his name, has two words totalling 16 characters in his name. Interestingly enough "Georgetown" has ten letters as does Washington (W did not exist in the Latin alphabet if I remember correctly). So we are up to 616 now – which is where some older versions of the Bible stop counting (ie 666 is 616 in reality). Interestingly, 616 is a virtual Pi cycle number! 4) DC has a strange system of labelling streets – after letters of the alphabet. There is an "L" street and in Latin numerology L=50. So, if some huge new bureaucracy opens up in DC with the avowed aim of making sure that US citizens have to have a number before they can buy or sell anything (cashless society comes to fruition??), then maybe it is on "L" street.

If so, we now have 666. This is not yet however, but something I am looking at. If all of this is correct, then this is how 666 comes about, as my best guess. Note also, according to Revelations, that 666 is the number of a man. Yep! It certainly is, although I do not believe that America's first president would appreciate this fact very much!

SEGMENT FOUR

CHAPTER TWO

THE CASHLESS SOCIETY (AHHH ... WHO NEEDS PAPER MONEY ANYWAY?)

Yeah ... a society where computers dominate and we do not have the "filthy lucre" (aka cash money – dollar bills) in our pockets. Sounds good right? Well it does at least until the computer breaks down at the store and you can't buy groceries, or a child's favourite confection when s/he is screaming so loudly that you can barely hear yourself think and other customers are staring daggers at you!

Ah, the joys of modern North American life! At least in this example you can buy your way out of the store with some soiled (but valid) bank notes and these NEVER "go down" or suffer from an unplanned power outage in a savage storm.

Yes, we can make all sorts of comments along these lines, but the fact of the matter is the trend and this is that every few years computer abilities double on a compound basis. The time is surely coming when profit-hungry bankers and desperately cash strapped governments will simply mandate that cash is no longer acceptable as a means of transacting business or (most importantly from their perspective), paying taxes of all sorts.

In my newsletter a few months ago I had a good look at all of this and wish to share with you my thoughts from that time (as they really haven't changed very much, if at all). Yes, I take awhile to seemingly get to the point, but have faith! I do get there and hopefully all will be made clear as I do.

What I am afraid of is that the powers-that-be in Washington have planned for a cashless society for a long time. Without advanced computers, this was impossible as there did not exist the storage technology to get all of hundreds of millions of individual transactions put through to the correct bank accounts in a timely manner. Clearly, if people did not have the faith to transact their business when the end result was anything less than assured, a move to a cashless system would be impossible. However, the miracles wrought by Messrs., Gates, Allen, Jobs et al., have done away with these fears just about completely it seems to me. The grip on the overall economy by the people who wish for this sort of thing to happen has tightened dramatically in just the past decade or so. All right then, without readers jumping up and down screaming "conspiracy nut – why did I waste my money in buying this book?", I must justify what I have been talking about. I hope I can, although I fear that many people will not accept whatever I write. Ok, I honour that, but at least give me the chance to try and get across my point.

There are many people who feel that there is a group of very well-to-do folk who wish to rule over us simply because "it is their right". They go by various names such as Illuminati, Octopus, Bilderbergers, you name it. Wealth begets power (I hope you will grant me that at any rate!) and if you are a multi-billionaire with few areas of the world left to conquer with your wealth in your chosen field, then it is believed (reasonable given human nature I think) that these people will try to go after absolute control over everything.

Wealth is a club and they know how to use it. This sort of behaviour has been known since the days of the prophets in The Old Testament and I quote the Book of Habakkuk Chapter 2, Verse 5 here when he talks about Death (with a capital "D", in other words the Devil) always looking for more and more souls to grab for himself. The relevant passage reads:- "Moreover, wealth is treacherous; the arrogant do not endure. They open their throats wide as Sheol; like Death they never have enough. They gather all nations for themselves, and collect all peoples as their own".

This is a pretty damning indictment, not so much on having wealth but having great financial accumulations and then not using them wisely. The Bible is filled with exhortations about helping the poor, the dispossessed, orphans, and widows, and yet while we do have the odd Bill Gates or Warren Buffett who are doing something with their incredible riches, I suspect that there are many, many others who care only about having "their throats open" and getting more and more no matter what misery they cause in so doing.

With great wealth comes great responsibility, but that is apparently unknown to so many; poor wretches (in the eyes of God) that they are. However we have to realise that over two thousand years ago the prophets in The Bible knew well what human nature would do with great wealth, and they wrote about it at length. Human nature does not change it seems and we must, in looking at how the hidden rich today use their wealth, understand this. If The Bible can give us a lot of lessons about Pi and Fibonacci, then why can it not do something similar in a blunt assessment of human nature?

So, the very well-to-do wish to extend their grasp of the world it seems. But what would they gain with all of this "cashless society talk" if/when it ever comes? All of the talk one sees on this subject tends to fall along the lines of control. Do you recall the controversy last Fall (2013) when JP Morgan/Chase bank was supposed to have placed limits on wires of money/assets leaving the USA? This was not followed up by other banks of any reasonable description and so, under pressure from coin dealers (if no one else), the bank backed down and we returned to the status quo ante when people forgot that this ever happened. Except that it DID happen although not permanently at that time. Was it some sort of trial balloon for use when a truly cashless society comes to pass? If what Chase had talked about ever came to pass on a more global scale across the US banking system (and how would that have affected the use of the US$ as the world's Reserve Currency I wonder?) then any and all securities transactions could have been easily monitored by virtually anybody looking to see what various rich Americans were doing. If somebody wanted to import a large number of silver or gold coins from abroad then this might be of great interest to various agencies wondering about the personal confidence (or lack of same) by some US citizens looking to diversify out of US$, at least to an extent.

As I said, this all came to naught ... at least for now! However as an old friend once told me (who had studied these things throughout his life) "With these people it is always two steps forward and one step back. Once they have come to a decision on what they are going to do, they do not back down or reverse their plans". OK, so if this IS the case, then the move towards cashless transactions will continue to grind inexorably onwards. What is the next step, and given what our Pi Cycle analysis has taught us so far it has to be quite quick. There have been some trial balloons floated, the most notable being that within the next few years people will have to have some sort of chip implanted into their arms so that they may be traced no matter where they go and no matter what they want to purchase and so forth.

When I was made aware of this, I wrote back to the person making these thoughts available and told him about the old ideas from the 1960s and 1970s when many "full blown nut cases" (as they were referred to back then) would advocate wearing a tin-foil hat when they went outside. This would be to avoid either having their mind read by orbiting satellites or to have some sort of ideas implanted by these same satellites. Given how far computer technology has come since the days when these wretched individuals told anybody and everybody about their concerns, maybe they weren't so far away from ultimate reality! The technology may not be able to be devised fast enough to suit the Pi Cycle timeline and at the same time have it accepted in large part by a very dumbed down population. So, given where we are today with credit cards, debit cards, and goodness knows what else, the ultimate rulers of our society (and I am sure they exist as Habakkuk wrote all of these centuries ago) will have to play on existing fears and outright paranoia which does not seem to be that far below the surface these days. What I suspect will happen is that cash will start to be demonised as "being fundamental to the financing of terrorism" or some such. At the same time Gold bullion will also come under increasing attack but, since the days of President Nixon severing the link between the US$ and Gold back in August 1971, this metal has been generally held in very low public esteem by Washington power brokers. The average American, as far as I can see, does not understand how Gold operates as a hedge and would, therefore, probably accept this line of reasoning being given to him/her.

In any event, control of your bank account (not to mention securities accounts) would be a welcome prize to those who seek it. Without cash, and only electronic access to your account, you are vulnerable to hacking and court ordered seizure on what could be rather flimsy evidence. Today, if you feel really threatened, you can withdraw a decent sized amount of cash and spend it as required. Yes, I know all about the official condemnation of large amounts of cash as being de facto evidence of your being a drug smuggler or some sort of tax dodger and I didn't say that living off large amounts of cash would be easy, but it is theoretically doable. This option is completely removed with an electronic form of banking. Look at things this way. Today people are told, relentlessly, that various US security organs can track every word you write/text/email/whatever. There is no privacy left and it seems as though the US court system is not going to stand in the way of this at all. The war against terrorism will not be lost because of some legalistic mumbo-jumbo seems to be the message. Well, if all of this is true with your communications, why is it such a long leap of faith to see that this can also be done with your bank accounts and so forth? It isn't.

So, if we have some sort of false flag event (and this could be a type of illness which, it is claimed, can be traced to "old and diseased banknotes") whereby the US authorities can start to withdraw said forms of paper money, then it will happen. People will be frightened to use cash for fear of "getting sick" and so they won't and will actually demand that cash be severely restricted or even removed from circulation! In fact, come to think of it, I now favour some such illness claim as a way to get banknotes removed! No muss, no fuss!

For those people who live overseas and who use paper money rather extensively, we might even have cell phones act as a form of "no cash banks". Don't laugh! I read (courtesy of the highly respected German daily Der Spiegel) that there are people in Rwanda, East Africa, (of genocide fame from only a few years ago) who are working hard on designing this technology so that people in very remote areas of that country can use their cell phones to buy and sell! It also seems that many African countries have a higher penetration of cell phone usage and possession than the United States itself! If it can be done in Africa, it can be done anywhere is probably the message we can take away from this. In US dominated Europe (culturally if nothing else) it would be a fairly easy sell I would think.

If paper money equals disease with a high probability of death in the USA, why would that logic not hold true in the very federalised EU?? It would hold true, which would mean that in a very short period of time paper money in the West might become passé. Now for my comments in the newsletters of a few months ago. At the end of these, I wish to write a small piece on how this ultimately unfolds. (These newsletter comments are a few paragraphs down).

HINT: Given that this is The End Times and that it involves the US and the US$, we are looking at something truly draconian developing. Go The Book of Revelation again please. Now look at the description of "666". It must be (again, if all my suppositions are correct) the ultimate control mechanism and I have broken this down so you can see how it comes about. It IS based on the name of a man, George Washington (!!). The average person is to be damned, according to The Book of Revelation, for taking this "666" mark willingly and worshipping the issuer of the mark. I do not wish to see scores of millions of Americans condemned in the eyes of God for taking this mark when they haven't a clue as to what it could be and are (most probably being told to believe this) that it is merely a simple way to "take care of your money with the absolute security of the US Government behind it. No muss, no fuss, no terrorism, no drugs, no drug trade, and it is all to make your life a lot simpler". We shall probably be told that a "mark is much easier to handle because, unlike a piece of paper which could be stolen or lost, the mark can never be lost or 'cannot be found' ". Please consider all of this very carefully. I do not claim to be some sort of "all-knowing" person when it comes to this or anything else for that matter. What I am is a long term trader who knows how to follow a trend very well. The cashless society is just such a cultural and societal trend. I am following it. I have come to "666" and wish to warn you as explicitly as I can. Plan your lives as though cashlessness is a done deal and is coming soon. It is. I expect this, using Pi Analysis, for it to be here by 2024/2025 at the latest (ie 2014 War Cycle Year, plus 11 - yep! that number again!). Do not enter into this blindly now! THINK!!! Now for the newsletters which I wrote on this, for your perusal:-

"I have been thinking about this for sometime now and while, with the continuing advances in computer science this is going to happen, I have to make sure that I do not seem to be like some sort of frothing-at-the-mouth radical with my views. I do not believe that this is to be the case here, and I shall simply follow the money to see where it leads in the principal circumstance. "The main thing to note here is that the US federal government (as a useful proxy for other 'advanced' governments around the world) is running deficits which are of the most mind-boggling dimensions, seemingly each and every year. The total debt is, as of today's date, November 15, 2013, is a staggering $ 17.1 trillion. "The rate of accumulation of this debt is not going to slow down, in my view, as increasing trends such as this usually have a blow-off of some sort in a short period of time. Marty Armstrong (yep, him again!) is on record as showing us that as of October 2015 the debt becomes so bad that there is a global revulsion for government/sovereign debt, and this is now less than two years away. My own Biblical analysis, presented for your consideration recently, shows almost exactly the same thing. "Reluctantly (as the implications are so bad) I have to agree with Armstrong as I trust I made clear in these recent Biblical analyses. For once, at that time, the US financial nay-sayers who have been wrong for literally decades now, will have their day in the sun. How high will this 'blow off' number finally reach before it all comes tumbling down? "If we have a decent sized war followed by an enhanced economic slowdown, then it is not impossible for us to see a figure of perhaps $ 30 trillion before the general revulsion for these sorts of numbers forces some sort of global buyers strike for US paper (and hence probably other over-indebted nations securities as well).

"So, what has this got to do with a cashless society? Well, it has everything to do with it actually! It has been written in several forums that the US tax gatherers are very concerned that people who deal in cash are not going to report their full and complete incomes, and hence not be charged the proper tax rates. "Over the years there have been many laws passed against people dealing in cash who are made to feel that they are doing something 'dirty and improper' somehow. This 'war on cash' does not seem likely to abate with the large and growing deficits, and the logical conclusion is that ALL cash will have to be withdrawn from circulation at some point, probably in the not too distant future. "One can say that there is to be a fairly severe element of control here. If a society cannot spend as it wishes (collectively) because the powers-that-be do not trust the citizens to be honest and forthright, then we are looking at a society which probably has, at best, a limited future. How is this so? To have a pure cashless society where everything and anything is overseen, means that all is monitored by computers of ever increasing complexity.

"Today, I saw something which made me wonder just how far down this particular path we are going to travel. A new series of algorithms has been discovered in Toronto in which computers can assess "1s" and "0"s and assess them at the same time as opposed to having a choice between the two possibilities. (I am not a computer guru by the way!). "Apparently this boosts computing power by large amounts which, in turn, suggests that it is coming along at just the right time to be the control mechanism for a future cashless society.

(Interesting, isn't it, how these things always seem to come together just when they are needed?). "In extremis, we can say that the Biblical '666' (or '616' if you wish, see below) is the ultimate cashless society code for control over what assets you have and how you spend them. I visited this theme in a recent newsletter on Revelation, and I do not see what is incorrect with it. It follows the money and seems to be a logical extension to where we are going. "If we have a federal database which tracks what every citizen is doing financially, then such a database (presumably run out of Washington DC, as that also seems to be the direction in which we are headed) could be easily modified to prevent anybody who is in not in favour with the federal government from buying or selling anything at all. An average person will have a mark on the right hand or forehead (perhaps even a tattoo for the 'gotta be with it crowd') which might read 'DC 999-99-9999 L' with one's coded Social Security number being the digits.

"It would be machine readable, clearly, and be marketed as something which is a natural outgrowth of the changes in society over the past generation or so, and which would (of course) 'place a crippling burden on the terrorists and drug dealers'. It would be something to 'make us all that much safer' in other words. I believe that this would sell, and sell fairly easily. "Well, what about the drug trade, which I would have thought would be the ultimate cash only trade? Some years ago this was estimated to be something like 5% of the US economy, which would amount to $ 750 billion – $ 1 trillion today. This a gargantuan sum of money and an unbelievable stack of $ 100 bills if indeed drugs are still traded in this manner. "An article in the German daily, Der Spiegel, told of how the drug flow works. It seems to start in the growing fields of Columbia and then makes it way through Panama and Mexico to the US in Texas. It then runs to New York and then to Europe. It pays the growers some EUR 3,000/ kg and the price in the EU runs from EUR 30,000 to EUR 90,000/ kg which is quite a mark-up!

"It is clearly very profitable, although not without risks, and I simply cannot see this being closed down because someone in Washington gets it in their heads to stop all cash transactions. In other words, in the real world, there are too many important wheels greased with this money for it to be stopped. If it is, then what can be used as a cash substitute? I do not know. Readers, if this cashless society dream/nightmare becomes reality, what do you think? "However, this sort of transaction lies at the periphery of society in the final analysis. If there is to be a major crisis developing in the US (and hence the world because of the liquidity significance of US Treasury securities) then the general weaknesses of the current US financial system will come swiftly to light. "I am referring to the huge US trade imbalance, whereby (it seems to me) that US companies manufacture all sorts of goods in China or other third World nations to be shipped back to the US. It is a short-sighted approach to making the proverbial quick buck and at some point the US$ rate of exchange will have to suffer and suffer badly. This is not yet however.

"The yawning budget deficit is unlikely to be addressed as far as I can see as we are approaching the 'blow off' point noted a day or so ago here. Overall, the Tea Party will probably be proven correct with their fears of a runaway accumulation of US federal debt in my view: for whatever good that will do in a strict economic sense. "The biggest problem will be the private pension funds which are now being crucified with their holdings of US Treasury certificates which yield nearly nothing in returns. I shall be re-examining this issue early in the new year, but my guess at this preliminary stage is that these funds will be nationalised so that 'our older citizens pensions can be made secure and worry free'.

"People who fear a nationalised health care system in the US today are going to be shown to have nothing to worry about here given what can happen with pensions! "The point is that when the well-to-do see the sorts of disasters starting to unfold with Treasuries and the economic infrastructure breaking down, they will want to run with whatever they can take with them – money wise. At that time (as I mentioned in the series of exchange controls which look to be being initiated by Chase bank) this action will probably be too late. "At that time, running with cash money will not be possible as far as I can see as we might be just about cashless overall. In other words, running with a lot of cash to Canada to send money wherever, will not be that viable a proposition. Wiring money to a major centre overseas from home will also be tracked and probably blocked by the Fed or Treasury. You will have left it too late! "If you are going to do anything of a precipitous nature, then take your lesson from investment guru Jim Rogers and his move to a nice apartment in Singapore a year or so ago. With a major US$ crisis (crises) brewing, I can tell you from watching Europe in the 1970s that all of the dollars (in this case) will be blocked from leaving the US, and the benefit thereby to the US economy will be that the US$, which then cannot be sold overseas, will thus be spent/invested in the US. How's that for the stuff which I used to do in my real working life?! (Hint: the US$ exchange rate will not take the pounding it would have were there no exchange controls).

"So, let's try to sum all of this up. I have never liked a cashless society as one always has to worry about going to the grocery store and seeing a sign to the effect 'Sorry, our computers are down'. With cash this cannot, of course, happen. "With US$ cash, one can always take a trip overseas as US$ cash is always welcome because the US$ is the reserve currency of the world (however long that lasts with any distortions which transpire during the transition to a cashless domestic society). This welcome will all be gone and one risks a 'Sorry, cash only, our computers do not accept domestic US cash cards'. Every penny you have will be in a bank (never under the mattress) or a securities or real estate account and therefore at risk of some sort of seizure on any pretext. "You cannot control your own future and the time will come (as noted in a previous essay, I am thinking 2024/25) when a very nasty controlling agency in Washington will simply say that unless you have a 'DC 999-99-9999 L' account marked on your forehead or right hand (when we shall be told that 'this prevents you losing a paper card or having it stolen – it is for your protection') you cannot buy or sell anything which is not approved for you. You will have nothing at all! "Now the only question is how fast this will all play out. My guess is that if you have financial assets you will be amazed at how fast you no longer have any control over a decent portion of them! Be prepared: it is coming!".

End of newsletter quotes. Now let's finish off this chapter by seeing exactly what "666" (OK, or "616") really is and how it is derived in today's modern world.

What has been written above (for the first three newsletter updates and today) is a fair sized chunk of material to be absorbed, at the very least. There is a lot of conjecture which may be dismissed by the reader as "imaginative" and so forth and I appreciate this divergence of opinion. Fair enough, but there remains just one more idea to place before you which can prove all of this when the time finally comes. How does "666" actually work, if it indeed does refer to Washington DC? Here is my interpretation on what an increasingly authoritarian Washington bureaucracy might try as it struggles to maintain a hold on an increasingly restive, rebellious, population.

Hint: watch for something to happen on "L" Street in DC as we move towards a system where "people cannot buy nor sell without the Mark/Number of The Beast on their right hand or forehead". Have a look and remember "L" street for a new bureaucracy dealing with this sort of (cashless society!) transactions.

Consider this-

1) If "666" refers to tightened financial and cultural control in the US, then Washington DC must be involved. 2) D=500 in Latin numerology; C= 100. So DC = 600. 3) George Washington, the founder of the city which bears his name, has two words totalling 16 characters in his name. Interestingly enough "Georgetown" has ten letters as does Washington (W did not exist in the Latin alphabet if I remember correctly). So we are up to 616 now – which is where some older versions of the Bible stop counting (ie 666 is 616 in reality). Interestingly, 616 is a virtual Pi cycle number! 4) DC has a strange

system of labelling streets – after letters of the alphabet. There is an "L" street and in Latin numerology L=50. So, if some huge new bureaucracy opens up in DC with the avowed aim of making sure that US citizens have to have a number before they can buy or sell anything (cashless society comes to fruition??), then maybe it is on "L" street.

If so, we now have 666. This is not yet however, but something I am looking at. If all of this is correct, then this is how 666 comes about, as my best guess. Note also, according to Revelations, that 666 is the number of a man. Yep! It certainly is, although I do not believe that America's first president would appreciate this fact very much!

SEGMENT FOUR

CHAPTER THREE

WIND POWER – YET ANOTHER
BAG OF HOT AIR?? (GUESS WHAT
I AM GOING TO SAY HERE!)

And now let me pass along to another great hope for the future of our energy hungry society and that is Wind Power. Yes, when someone first mooted this as a possible solution to the "energy crisis", we all heard come-backs of "Hot air" or some such! However the powers-that-be (great debaters one and all – sorry I really do have a bee in my bonnet about the UN, don't I?) said otherwise.

We were then all treated to visions of old fashioned Dutch windmills from centuries past and were told that a modern version of this would use all of the free energy from moving air. In turn, this would power small generators in the windmills to churn out all of the electricity that a modern society could ever want or need! We were all told that the Free Market would find the solutions we all needed and life would go on as before. All we needed was the right incentive and lots of government money in the form of grants and the like. In other words, we should throw money at the problem willy-nilly and simply hope that some of it sticks! Now, as you may have gathered by now, I am a big believer in government intervention for the simple reason that governments never have to worry what shareholders think: when something has to be done which is very expensive, a proper intervention policy would save uncounted amounts of money.

I am going to wander off subject for a paragraph or two to make a point, which I hope will come back to illustrate what we have found to be the fallacies of Wind Power(!). Yep! you read that one correctly! This one doesn't work either, but that will not stop The Great Debaters from simply declaring that this is what we have to look forward to and that it "will" work! Anyhow, for the point at issue immediately, let me revert back to nuclear power here and what Germany is doing to phase out this ghastly electricity generating medium. To dispense with this wretched nuclear subject (finally!) and return to Wind Power with the above lessons learned, I refer you to one simple thing which was used in the United States to sell nuclear energy to an ever gullible American public (sorry if you take offense at these words, it is just a fact of life at least with nuclear power). We were told, and I remember this from when I was much younger, that nuclear power would make "electricity too cheap to even monitor". I don't know about you, but I am still waiting for my first electric bill reading "Amount Due – $ 0.00". The sheer absurdity of this statement must make one wonder.

Why would any company even consider getting involved with such a method of generating electricity when the returns, by definition, must be zero? Why didn't people and slippery politicians even think to ask such simple questions? Now the questions are MUCH more difficult and are probably beyond response. We now see "MUCH more difficult questions" arising amidst the obvious shortcomings over Wind Power. So to return to Wind Power, and its initially great expectations, we should be able to look at the EU for a good guide as to where this area of experimentation is going. Why should this be anyhow? Well, after the Falkland Islands (with an average wind speed of about 20 mph all day) the windiest pace on the planet is located at Horn's Reef, Denmark (a member of the EU). With the constant flow of wind from the sea, this was thought to be a no-brainer for Denmark to be a leader in Wind Power technology.

It turns out that the powers-that-be did not fully understand what was happening when they jumped all over this particular bandwagon thinking that it was the proverbial "sure thing" (as is there is ever such an animal!). Well, as is with the case with Solar Power, it turns out that Windpower is also "less than functional". In other words, it really doesn't work either from a monetary perspective or from a mechanical/theoretical analysis. Sigh! Somethings never change do they?

With EU governments pouring money into Wind Power and great columns of windmills being constructed across the North Sea, the feeling was that this was something which would prove its worth. Great subsidies were also paid out to landowners who leased large tracts of their properties to up and coming companies (Wind Power, of course!) who were anxious to prove what they could do in this new "modern age". I wondered at the time (using the British model as Britain has a great number of wind/gales from Autumn/Winter storms) how such huge subsidies could be factored into the final price structure for the end product of these windmills. It can't; at least if it wishes to be competitive with other power sources (including Solar Power!). Nevertheless, the EU plodded on with their plans.

Finally, the German press stood up and told the world that the Horn's Reef project was a colossal waste of money and could not possibly work. If we follow the money, always a good path in assessing a new technology, we see that (as noted previously) that the EU wishes to go back to fracking: about as un-renewable a source of energy as one can get. What was found in these articles was that in setting up the windmills in the North Sea, the planners did not seem to have factored into their calculations the corrosive effects of salt water on wind mills which may stand idle for some periods of time when the wind does not blow as projected. (Which Grade School did they get their engineers from, I must somewhat acerbically ask?). They also found that winds blow mainly at night in that area of the world and, surprise surprise, most people in Denmark and neighbouring areas of Germany are asleep at that time and use very little of the power being so generated! Then they found out that when electricity WAS being generated there was no good way to store it for when it would be required by the consumers. In other words, Denmark might be able to generate all sorts of power from the North Sea, but it was effectively useless!

The German would-be consumers were angry and had to turn to other sources for their electricity (nuclear power raises its ugly head here!) and billed, under contract, the Danes for the difference between their non-existent power and traditional nuclear energy. So, from a "sure thing" where there would be pots of money for all concerned (see my comments on nuclear power some paragraphs back, - now do you see why I had to reintroduce this loathsome subject again a few paragraphs ago?) the Danes actually found a way to lose on the deal! Amazing! As far as I know the problems here have not yet been resolved. The only place where windmills have worked has been in the Falkland Islands where power can be generated twenty-fours a day given the wind flows down there. As an aside here, one must compliment the planning department of the Falklands Government in Port Stanley. Someone there noticed that as a British Crown Colony it is considered part of Great Britain. This being the case, the Falklands should be eligible for a generous subsidy from Brussels! Anyhow, on the basis of "nothing ventured, nothing gained" they applied for this subsidy on these grounds and ... got it!! So the EU is subsidising a place which is about as far away from the EU as one can get. The farmers who use this facility to supplement their electricity generation on the very remote farms down there are doing very well, I understand, versus the huge diesel costs which they had to pay previously with inefficient generators. Well, I'm glad this works in at least one area of the EU anyway! Too bad it cannot be used elsewhere in the EU as the wind, as noted, is simply generated at the wrong time versus the customers who need it. (Solution: move the EU to the Falklands??).

Other problems noted with windmills (British windmills here) was that there was too much wind! These windmills have a safety factor which shut them down when wind speeds exceed a certain limit – I believe this is 100 mph. In some of the really severe gales there, this has been exceeded and has resulted in jammed motors, locked windmill blades and fires started on occasion when the motors simply could not handle the stresses.

I also saw, in the British press, pictures of windmills being knocked down by sheer pressure of air flows from such storms. It seems to me that windmills lying on the ground, in flames, are not going to generate that much in the way of electricity! British landowners also found out (in their crazed greed for easy money from the government) that the sheer noise from blades turning at high speeds can ruin a decent night's sleep and make living anywhere near these wretched devices very difficult indeed! Another problem which was found was that windmills and migratory birds simply do not mix well: unless you like seeing bits of birds which look like they have been strained through a giant sieve.

The EU and the UK are not the only places with windmill problems. I am fortunate enough to receive the updates, issued from time to time, by the legendary oilman T. Boone Pickens of the United States. Now up in his 80s, he is still looking for new technologies and ways to make money from them. It seems, to this writer, that he also has what is quite rare for any entrepreneur these days and that is a love of his country and to do what is right to keep it on top, which means solving its growing energy difficulties. For quite sometime he has been championing the cause of Wind Power as an answer to a major part of America's energy woes. In his letter to his "Army", he trumpeted America's staggering wind potential as he saw it and boldly proclaimed that wind coming off the Pacific Ocean into the Pacific North West (and California one presumes) would make the US "The Saudi Arabia of Wind Power". I am not sure what the Falkland Islands would say about this; ditto Horn's Reef; and ditto Alberta's own Pincher Creek (the third windiest place on the planet)! Anyhow he did what he considered his due diligence and got to the point where he told his "Army" one day that he was going to meet some apparently very influential people in Washington DC about what he wanted to do to start his plans of operation. He was optimistic and thought that he would get some sort of subsidy to back up his claims and plans. Given that this is how things get done in the United States, and how many advanced nations elsewhere in the world have handled this approach, I suppose that he was not being unrealistic. Well, he went to Washington, saw his people and ... came home with precisely zero in funding or grants!

He said nothing about what happened (or rather not happened), but as this was taking place at about the time that the EU was seeing the problems with Wind Power I think he was told that he had better forget the whole thing because it didn't work, either financially or technically.

It must have been a bitter blow given the effort he put into what he believed was correct. I do not believe that Washington was given a strong financial incentive by the oil companies to shoot him down. It is what it is, and Boone simply struck out. Now he talks about oil and the various ways that this can be better used to "make America energy independent". I can't see this given the very limited life span of fracking, but that is what he is talking about: energy from whatever petroleum based source which can be found and accessed.

In looking at this dismal subject (Wind Power that is!) I should look at the Danish company Vestas. In many respects this is like what we saw with the US company FSLR (Vestas is traded on the Pink Sheets in NY under the symbol VWSYF, FYI!). It started out life as if people could not get enough of what was on offer – so great was the belief that this, indeed, was time to get involved with alternative energy and Wind Power. The stock soared to DKK 690 or so in 2009 ($1 = 5.5 DKK – Danish Kroner; Denmark being one of the few countries in the EU to still use its own currency and not the Euro). Then we started to see the stories about technical problems with windmills and the unique (but nonetheless valid) worries about off-shore sited windmills. The price of the stock crashed and at its low point it traded at something like US$ 4/DKK 22: quite a drop from DKK 690. Worries about the financial stability of the company (despite the vast sums available to it from the Danish and EU Governments) surfaced and the CEO was forced out. Now, did what happened with FSLR happened with Vestas? Did it bounce off the bottom?

Yes it did! Currently (May 20, 2014) it is trading at about DKK 270/280 with the trading patterns on the charts looking very bullish indeed. Personally, I would not chase after this stock if I wanted to buy it but would wait for some sort of pullback and then scale in purchases. Your mileage may vary! So, given that it has traded in a very similar pattern to FSLR what can we say about the underlying fundamentals? Regrettably, people are once again buying because "if we don't, everyone else will buy". So, when everyone else staggers off the edge of the cliff, you are going to do so as well? Apparently this is the case.

The Debating Society Extraordinaire in NYC has again decreed that (well, effectively so anyway) that "Wind Power must be made to work" and so, because the "great thinkers" have decreed this, the lemmings rush to buy Vestas (VWSYF) as fast as they can because it must obviously be a money spinner! These same people might hate the concept of the UN with a passion, but when an alternative energy decree comes out of those intellectually clogged corridors, they rush to buy. They are caught in the idea of "Let's make money anyway we can, whether we understand it or not!".

SEGMENT FIVE

SO WHAT IS HAPPENING (AFTER ALL WE HAVE WRITTEN)? ... OR... GERRY, WHAT IS GOING TO "GET US" IN THE FINAL ANALYSIS?

CHAPTER ONE

◆◆◆◆◆

IS THE STATE DEPARTMENT CORRECT? CAN IRAN START THROWING NUKES AROUND?

All kidding aside (and in this book I have tried, from time to time to use the lighter touch a bit) we now have to sum up what has gone before in this book for the final segment. We have seen what I hope is interesting Pi Analysis from The Bible which should make you think and wonder if what it forecast could well be what some of the doom sayers are calling for. In Segment Two we have had a long look at what I sincerely believe lies ahead for Canada (and Western Canada – ABC Land) against a voracious raw materials appetite from a famished US. Will the US be able to "Chomp, chomp" its way to fulfillment without having to devour her neighbours?

Sadly, I do not think so. Then in the last segment, Segment Three, we have had what I think is a decent look at what constitutes many forms of alternative energy and why nearly all of them are failures and will probably soon be so. We could also, in this segment, have a look at something which the Japanese are supposed to be interested in and that is Solar Power, but with a twist.

According to The Japan Times this morning (May 27, 2014) Japan wants to launch a huge array of very large satellites which will capture the sun's rays and microwave them to Earth to be used as electricity to replace nuclear power, among others. As I recall, this was discussed decades ago and it was thought that it belonged in the realm of science fiction, and that was that!

However, no matter what you believe as regards alternative energy forms and their potential for adding to our staggering energy/electricity requirements, the fact remains that we are going to need lots of ways to generate power and, additionally, to cut back on the supposedly demonic use of fossil fuels (ie coal, oil, and so forth). We have been looking at Wind Power, Solar Power and allied items and the situation is not going to get any better with people running around playing politics and always claiming that "we have the solution" – whether "we" is a nation or company, big or small. So, given this, what is the true state of affairs in the world anyhow? How have global societies constructed themselves for what is clearly the end game in power generation? The big question I have, of course is The Question. Way back when in the first stages of this book, I wrote a rather flattering article on Marty Armstrong. Not that he doesn't deserve it of course, but one of the points I raised was his discovery of the grisly War Cycle which comes to a 25 year peak in 2014 (that's this year!). How will war affect the very delicate political and economic situation around the world? We have to include the economic situation, of course, as what happens there can cause massive upsets in global derivative markets and the world's interest rate structure.

I cannot write about every nation as I simply do not want to continue writing about the large number of societies existing on our globe and not be finished by next Christmas! There are several hot spots on our planet and these will probably suffice for a quick analysis or so as any real problems there will drag in the major powers with who knows what effect on everybody else. The US rants and rails against Iran and how it has developed nuclear weapons for use against its Arab neighbours. Iranians are NOT Arabs by the way, and are Shi'ite Muslims versus the Sunni sects which largely dominate the entire region outside that country. Sunnis and Shi'ites hate one another with a rare passion, and one only has to think back to the "Sectarian troubles in Northern Ireland" a generation or so ago when Roman Catholics and Protestants came close to a civil war over this issue.

It was embarrassing for London (Northern Ireland is part of the UK) and the Vatican, home to Roman Catholicism, has been trying to bring the rival churches together for many years now. Nevertheless Sunni-Shi'ite violence has happened and so we can at least understand why various branches of a supposedly solid religion such as Islam can come to blows very easily. Mr.Paul Craig Roberts writes a quite extraordinary series of newsletters quite frequently these days and has written on the subject of Iranian nuclear weapons once, quoting an amazing story from The Afghan Times which I wrote a long newsletter on at the time. I would like to reproduce it for you now:-

"Well, I have finally screwed up my courage and started to think seriously about something which should not be – The Islamic Republic of Iran having a cache of nuclear weapons and what has happened around the world with that knowledge being clearly imprinted on so many diplomats' and leaders' minds. First see http:// kabulpress.org/my/spip.php?article85229 . Yes, this is a newspaper published in Kabul, Afghanistan and at first I looked at the URL and winced. "I wondered about the sort of rubbish which might come out of that war-torn city, but as it was recommended by Paul Craig Roberts in his most recent letter of November 13, I felt I had to give it at least a look-see. I am glad I did. This story, together with a large number of others referenced on the same page, contains more information than I had ever thought possible. Clearly there is no press censorship in Kabul! The authors seem to have a lot of knowledge based on previous life experience and from what I know of the subjects being discussed, they are not wrong with what they write. See this cut from one of their subsidiary stories – Iran's nuclear weapons programme- "EXCLUSIVE: Iran's Black Market Nuclear Warheads Are an Open Secret "They continue to restrain Western military action "Saturday 22 October 2011, by Matthew J. Nasuti

"On March 21, 2008, this author was among a group of Foreign Service officers and diplomats who received a briefing at the State Department on Iran. The Department's Middle East expert, under questioning by this author, told the group that it was 'common knowledge' in the region that Iran had acquired tactical nuclear weapons from one or more of the former Soviet Republics. Using the vague term 'common knowledge' allowed the expert to discuss the information in an unclassified presentation. "This disclosure was consistent with reports that have been circulating for years. On April 9, 1988, the Jerusalem Post reported that Iran had acquired four tactical nuclear weapons from Kazakhstan. The Post cited Iranian documents obtained by the Israeli government and authenticated by U.S. Congressional investigators. In March 1992, 'The Arms Control Reporter' published an article confirming that Iran had acquired four nuclear warheads from Russia. "A May 1992, report in 'The European' claimed that Iran had acquired two nuclear warheads from the former Soviet republic of Kazakhstan. These reports were all generally confirmed in a 2002 interview given by General Yuri Baluyevsky, then Russia's Deputy Chief of Staff. A report in the Cleveland Jewish NEWS dated January 27, 2006, reported that there were 20 sites in Iran in which dispersed tactical nuclear warheads were being stored. (Portion only of entire story)".

I can see the comments now about "Gerry stop being so much of a chump. Isn't it obvious that anybody can write this sort of stuff, and in case you hadn't noticed this is more than two years old". To this I merely state "so what"? We are looking at a long term trend here which goes back decades to the time of the Shah of Iran and it is quite conceivable that this article is just one of an ongoing series of updates. However, what can be gleaned from this story is that the Western powers take their time to react, and so they have done in this instance. How many times have we seen "scary stories" about Iran doing devilish things with their enrichment programmes? How many times has Israel cried for "something to be done" about this apparent wickedness in Tehran? How many times have we seen (well, I certainly have!) stories that "within six months Iran will have a bomb"? Quite a few over the last decade I would say. Let us continue with the newsletter on this very dangerous subject:-

"The West has reacted in several ways. First, they have slapped Iran with all sorts of sanctions as regards its economy. Its oil cannot be paid for in "US$, but that so far has not been that much of a burden overall". Secondly, there are all sorts of diplomatic sanctions in place. In the grand scheme of things (nukes versus everything else) these sanctions do not amount to much more then the proverbial hill of beans. How can they? "However, in following the money (my favourite system for assessing things as it relies on greed and human nature, which never fail!) we see that there are tell-tale signs that what Iran is doing IS in fact the truth and that the Kabul Press is clearly privy to a great deal of information which is not that widely disseminated in the Western press. What could these signs be? "Initially, the most obvious reason is that despite a huge number of threatened attacks on the Islamic republic, nothing has ever been done. Why should this be so? Clearly, if Iran has nuclear weapons, an attack on that large country which 'did not get them all' would invite a retaliation of some description. "This would not come in the form of a Shahab-4 missile aimed at London or Washington but rather at the oil fields of Saudi Arabia or the Middle East in general. Why shouldn't they react in this manner? I believe it was one of the Afghan leaders who came up with the idea that America cannot be beaten in a direct military showdown (most probably correct) but that the way to attack the USA would be economically. "This could be done via staging a series of brushfire wars in Central Asia (ie Iraq and Afghanistan) which would be waged using guerilla tactics. These would cost the US a staggering amount of money. Looking at the overall US debt burden's increase in the past decade or so, this seems quite correct. If your enemy tells you how he is going to defeat you, why would you not pay attention? "If the prospect of your enemy doing a great more damage to your now weakened economy via damaging your most precious import (ie oil), then you have a real worry on your hands! Overall this in fact is quite a threat and I am inclined to believe that Washington/EU is not going to go too far down that particular path - that is to say attacking Iran's nuclear weapons and risking a collapse in your over-indebted, over-leveraged, economy. "It also explains something else which has been irritating me for sometime now, and which I wrote about to an energy newsletter some time ago. In assessing this, in that letter, I was taken by the fact that all major discoveries were being guarded zealously. "In particular with the discoveries of what may be mega-deposits in the Falkland Islands (which I have more than a nodding acquaintance over) London is going as far as building an airport on remote St. Helena Island in the South Atlantic which could apparently handle military flights going south to Port Stanley/Mt. Pleasant in the Falklands. The short shrift given to wretched Argentina over the issue was most noteworthy. Why, I asked? "China has threatened to nearly come to blows with Japan over the riches of the South China Sea. China has also bought into the Tar Sands in Alberta, and I had considered this a normal asset play for its national balance sheet. Now the answers are clear and obvious and the money trail can only lead to the Middle East. "If the feeling in major global capitals is that Iran could 'really wreck the joint' then any and all discoveries will be guarded with great definition. Another way of putting this would be to say that these people are clearly 'in the know' about what Iran is capable of, consider it a very real probability, and are hedging their bets all down the line. Argentina and Japan are, in all probability, going to be left out in the cold. Iran is that serious. "What else can we say? It is known that the US is seriously considering the desirability of establishing an anti-missile base in Poland. This was announced well over a year ago, and the reason stated was that the EU would need this to protect itself from an Islamic Iran and a possible attack. The EU was quite content with this, but not so the Russians. "They seemed quite convinced that the proposed base was aimed at them, using the rather straightforward logic that an anti-Iranian base should be much closer to Iran than Poland. What was interesting here was that despite all sorts of references to Russia eliminating this base along the lines which President Kennedy threatened to do in the Cuban missile crisis in 1962, the US refused to back down. There were a few small givebacks to placate the Russians, but the overall idea is unmovable: the US will not back down. "So far, nothing of consequence has been heard from Moscow on all of this activity, but if President Putin is as closely linked with Iran as The West seems to think, then he knows full well what is happening and can only play the 'wounded Russian pride' card for so long. "The US was prepared to risk, in other words, a major confrontation with Moscow over what IS (in my opinion) an anti-Iranian base. Therefore, we can conclude that the Iranian threat is very real and is perceived as that in Western capitals. They are panicking and are probably right to do so. "Why would this be anyhow? The feeling in another edition of the Kabul Press is that Iran would have no scruples about selling these fiendish weapons to what the West calls terrorist groups. Has this happened, and Iran and/or these groups are engaging in all sorts of bluff and double bluff with Washington these days? I do not know - so far on at least a direct basis. "However, we can follow what is happening in Washington and see that the corridors of power there contain some truly frightened people. How do we know that? We simply look at what is happening in that country. Since the attacks on 9/11, we have seen a proliferation of security agencies develop there whose principal motive seems to be to find out absolutely everything which is written or spoken in the US at any one time. "Why would this be in the US of all places? The only answer which makes sense is that Iranian nukes are now loose in the world and as such the question can only be how many have been smuggled into the US. What threats has Washington received which makes American leaders react as they have? Surely there must have been some very nasty ones along the way! "Therefore, while many civil libertarians and right-wing bloggers are overtly hostile to TSA, DHS, and who knows what else, I am now thinking that they are wrong and that these new alphabet institutions really are devoted to stopping something awful from emerging in the US. "Yes, there is a real problem with what might be called 'mission creep' or the simple problem of senior bureaucrats looking to expand their empires before other agencies do. For instance, I see today (November 15) that the EPA, in a desire to expand their mandate to protect American waterways, may even wish to impede the private ownership of property! So where is the EPA going with all of this?

"It is not good and would ultimately result in State control of everything in the name of protecting the land, water, and, of course, people. I mention this as we have to look at what the TSA is doing as regards expanding their remit from simple airport inspectors to possessing armoured trucks and cars which can patrol highways looking for possible terrorists. The DHS and the 'Listening Agencies' have all been in the headlines recently both home and abroad spying on just about everyone (including the German Chancellor Merkel) to see what the terrorists are up to. "Where do they go from here anyway? Just how serious is the Iranian threat and does it justify this sort of 'mission creep' (or should we call it 'mission gallop')? The right wing blogs have been having a field day worrying that everything we are seeing has been put in place prior to some sort takeover attempt of the entire USA by a major entity. "The motive here would be in that taking over the USA would be actually saving it and making sure that it continues to exist as an independent entity which is safe from the Iranian threat. The same blogs have commented that Obama is very overmatched in his job (and one can see this in his physical deterioration since he has been in office). What I think they are saying (and this maybe nothing but rampant speculation on my part) is that in the current environment of an apparent failure of Obamacare, the Iranian threat, and the rapid growth of an all encompassing bureaucracy, that perhaps someone else could be found to take over this very demanding job. "It also appears that in the attempt to gain ever more control over their mandate, many Washington agencies are looking to take advantage of many unfortunate incidents which have been happening. I refer to the Boston marathon bombing where two Chechen immigrants to the US apparently set off a homemade bomb which caused many casualties. "The results in finding the one Chechen who eluded initial capture was that homes were searched in a systematic basis and the whole city was placed in a 'lockdown' type of mode. Many Constitutionalists objected to what happened but it seems to be a question of irrelevance. Bostonians did not object and in fact cheered the local police when the danger had passed. "This sort of civic reaction tells any and all who are watching that there is no problem for the average American in accepting additional bureaucratic encroachment, on the understanding that 'it makes us all safe'. There is to be no more boogeyman to imperil what Americans regard as their lifestyle and that is the bottom line to all of this. "Given that, in the thrust of this letter, we are seeing a genuine fear of what a really dedicated terrorist could do with a 'rogue nuke' in the US, the federal authorities are going to have their hands full. They really cannot afford to have a 'small' nuke (if one of these actually exists) explode in a major US city during, say, rush hour. "That would tell all and sundry that the alphabet agency clampdown is simply not working and that individual US citizens are not being protected. This may sound somewhat harsh given that many Iranian bombs may have been tracked down and removed from US society, but one will be all that it will take given the great veil of secrecy which prevails over the entire issue. "I would say, based on what has been written over the past few days, that if there is even one nuclear explosion in the US, that there will be a complete clampdown on anything and everything in the US. It would be foolish to expect that the relevant agencies have not drawn up plans should this nightmare ever occur. It may even be that events outside US borders would be impacted as well. "One of the things I have done for many years now is to research what the US might like to do if it felt it had the need to do so. On the US/Mexican border there is a fence and this is policed rather aggressively to stop Mexicans (and who knows who else) from coming into the US proper. There have also been articles which show that the US Border Patrol would like to have the authority to patrol within Mexico itself and to effectively control the area under a sort of cordon sanitaire. I do not think that this has happened or is going to happen anytime soon. However, if something disastrous happens in the US, courtesy of Iran then all bets may be off. "In Canada (which has the so-called, longest undefended frontier in the world, that with the US) we see something similar. Some years ago, there was apparently some sort of 'exchange agreement' between Canadian and American law enforcement to the effect that US police officers (from the various states) could patrol, with an RCMP escort, within Canada to a certain distance. "As far as I can recall, this must have been some sort of pilot programme as it was only undertaken East of Vancouver, British Columbia. I cannot recall Canadian police officers patrolling South of the border, which is interesting. Canadian motorists were pulled over fairly routinely and the whole practice wasn't formally exposed until one of the people being pulled over was an off duty Vancouver police officer who apparently took exception to being ticketed by a Texas patrolman! "What is of great interest to myself is that it does not seem to have been an agreement between governments, but rather between various national police forces only. The only logical conclusion one can make from all of this subterfuge was that there was a deeper purpose involved. In the light of what I have been writing, I therefore conclude that this 'agreement' was merely an extension of Washington police powers, and an extension which could well be used in a time of great emergency – an Iranian emergency. "Something along the lines of all of this was a cordon sanitaire reaching into Canada as well as Mexico. Old maps that I saw on-line suggest that the American authorities requested a 100 mile security buffer, which, as far as I saw, suggested that only the prairies would be affected. Later on this was reduced to 50 miles, but I have seen nothing further. Again, (and this may be completely true in Alberta with the huge Tar Sands deposits – a rich prize if the Iran thing gets out of control) I wonder about these sorts of what might be regarded as extreme planning". (End of long newsletter extract).

This is quite a lot of material for my readers to digest in just a few days. Looking at the quality of information in the Kabul Press, there may be other such analyses coming in the new year. Again (and you are probably tired of me saying this) next year is the 25 year cycle – the War Cycle of Armstrong and a correct one in my view. Looking at what we have been discussing over the past week or so, why is it so unreasonable to expect that this War Cycle will not play out as it has done often in the past? It could be that all of the previous threats against Iran were rebuffed because it simply "wasn't the time" for such things to work. If all that is so, then the mullahs in Tehran are going to have a big shock this time. It may be that the Saudis and the Israelis (now there's an unholy alliance for you!) will attack initially with the US (with all bills paid for by Riyadh, this is important for US budgetary reasons) picking up the residue. This may be how it is presented to Washington, but in war things seldom go as planned! We can confirm that with the mess in Washington from an overmatched Obama (to be frank I would suspect that virtually anybody else would have the same problem right about now) requires that something else be tried by The White House. The GOP is running all over the place laughing at the inept rollout of Obamacare, but they miss the point. The real problem in DC (which the leadership of the GOP should know all about as it is a long term difficulty) is Iran and terrorist groups with nuclear weapons. Right after this must be the very real problem with the budget and the quaintly American institution of the Debt Ceiling. These are critical issues to be sure (with the Debt Ceiling being far more significant) and if the GOP leadership does not understand these things, we are all in trouble! For Obama to go after a sideline/distraction war, he must market this properly to a jaded American public, and it must have something of real significance. Just look at the results of the Boston bombing noted above. It seems to this observer that Americans will sell their collective souls for a bit of short term safety and there are far too many people in Washington DC who are willing to give them what they want. If a war in the critical Middle East is just one more nail in this particular coffin, then so be it! It will not be hard to get the public onside for such a conflict, especially if it is said "The Saudis will pay for it all. There is no downside, and your safety will be assured". If there is any problem, then surely another what is called a false flag will put the quietus to any opposition. There WILL be a war in my view. The odds against it not happening are simply far too high. So, this is quite a bit bit of information from a couple of articles in a Kabul newspaper! Look for more, as noted before, simply because there are so many knock-on effects to be considered once the calendar rolls into 2014. Oh, one thing I forgot. If Iran IS using old Soviet nukes, then an explosion in a US city can be blamed on the Soviets (nuclear radiation signature) which is convenient as The Soviet Union no longer exists. Iran could claim that they are "blameless" in such a tragedy, but I wonder how that would play out in Washington?

SEGMENT FIVE

CHAPTER TWO

❖❖❖❖❖❖

ENOUGH ON IRAN, GERRY! OK, HOW DO YOU FEEL ABOUT NORTH KOREA (DPRK)

Let's ease into this a bit rather than hit you with a sudden change from Iran to the Democratic People's Republic of Korea (DPRK as just noted, or North Korea). The US, if one reads literally any newspaper, American or foreign, has a LOT of problems around the world. We have just had a long look at the intense problems that the US has with Iran (although, and wouldn't this be the ultimate in irony, if the US was forced to join forces with Iran against the ISIL insurgency forces in neighbouring Iraq?) and these are not going to go away at all.

Well, think about this please! If you were Iran's rulers and were faced with a VERY hostile US (not to mention Saudi Arabia) would you give up your nuclear weapons? I wouldn't as they are probably all that are standing between a belligerent State Department and national annihilation. This is the big problem for the US and it may be insoluble given that the US planners generally have a rather narrow timeline on the decisions they make. (Act in haste, repent at leisure?). To be frank, I have never been a great fan of the US State Department and what it is trying to do overseas. However, I make a large exception when it comes to Iran. The overthrowing of the Shah of Iran (and the "Peacock Throne") in 1979, was seen in Iran as the elimination of the man the US kept in power to make sure that Iran stayed firmly in the Western camp. Ayatollah Khomeini put an end to that in double quick time and the hatred of the United States there grew, culminating in the attack on the US embassy in that year as well. I do not believe that this attitude has changed and the chant of the Revolutionary Guards - "Death to America" - is still current.

The State Department is doing their job properly in the case of Iran, and if Iran DOES have the nuclear weapons, Washington would be criminally remiss not to have sanctions and defensive postures just about everywhere. On closing this comment about Iran one wonders about the price of oil and the Iranian nuclear threat. If Americans are groaning about gasoline prices with oil at its current (end May) level of $ 104; what do you think that the reaction will be if Iran uses one of its nukes on Saudi Arabia?

Do you now see why I devoted a full segment of this book to assessing "The Merger" between Canada and the US? There are simply so many variables to be considered in the oil markets these days, not to mention that COMEX market backwardations saying that we are in long period of shortages, that I do not believe these merger talks are going to go away. The need for the United States to secure long term supplies as quickly as possible is now paramount. It is entirely possible that the meeting of NAFTA heads of State in Mexico in February 2014 saw all of this laid before them in the simplest terms. Hillary Clinton, ever the opportunist, saw in this the possibilities of a much more integrated North American continent: Mexican labour; US manufacturing capacity; and Canadian natural resources. Again, as I have mentioned many times in the newsletter, there are far too many "interested parties" (shall we call them) for these merger talks not to continue on various levels.

We also have the problems in the Ukraine which are not going to go away as it looks like Russian President Putin is playing a masterful game in the Eastern part of that country. It looks to this observer that he is encouraging the Russian majority there to engage in a civil war with the Kiev Government (which came to power in elections after a coup – EuroMaidan as we all saw in the newspapers). The Ukraine is about as bankrupt as it is possible to get and is again finding problems in paying Russia for its Natural Gas from what I understand. Putin is going to grind the US and NATO down with endless low intensity war while goes after bigger game: probably in the Middle East. The State Department is tied down in two places therefore and now we may see DPRK being a third. As you will see in this chapter on DPRK, the US may be realising that it may have more on its plate than it can handle right now and looks to be playing nice with Pyongyang (capital and seat of power in North Korea) although there is a snag for Kim Jong-un's government there. What is this? Oh ... perhaps the US wants to eliminate DPRK by merging it with its southern neighbour?? As have alluded to earlier, the year 2014 (again quoting the work of Marty Armstrong) is a War Cycle year – specifically the danger period being August of this year. So, do we see a build up in the Middle East because of the Iranian threat with an explosion shortly after this month? I see nothing to indicate that this is happening and, in fact, President Obama is looking to get peace feelers going with the Iranian authorities. While many in the United States have condemned this "go soft" approach to Iran and favour something up to an including air strikes, this would be very bad indeed if there is a nuclear response. So, with this in mind, I do not favour the possibilities of a US-led attack on the country. The other possibility is something which might be done in the Ukraine if Washington feels that it has not got what it wants after the May 25 elections there. However, the feeling I get in watching the financial markets is that there is not much to play for in the Ukraine – and in fact never was, despite some rather bellicose statements which were made earlier on in the crisis. Well, if we aren't seeing a war (or a major change of political structure, which is the other part of Armstrong's War Cycle hypothesis) what DO we see then? My favourite candidate is one which has not been seen discussed yet. In other words there is no consensus as to what is to be done with this comical but very dangerous state: North Korea. After Japan had its colonialist butt kicked in 1945 when it took its shattering defeat we have seen 70+ years pass, and this time line will be complete in August (see above mentioned month in the Iran analysis above!) some 69 years ago.

Now 69 years is a Pi Cycle number as is 2014 interestingly enough. My bet, therefore, is that something rather extraordinary is about to happen in North Korea – or "Democratic People's Republic of Korea/DPRK" to give it its full name. I have been assessing this for quite sometime now and my feeling is that the question of oil will once again lead the way. I was told by a gentleman on a site I post to, that the US was in Viet Nam because there exists gobs of it near the Chinese border. Today (well in May anyway) we see the Chinese threatening to attack that area of Viet Nam because of poor treatment meted out to Chinese tourists there. In reality, I wonder. The US was not able to grab Vietnamese oil reserves in the long war it suffered there, and now what about China?? The US bears little love for Kim Jong-un's regime in Pyongyang, DPRK. It has piled sanction on top of sanction with the usual sanctimonious words such as "The international community is outraged at this, that, and so". This is usually in response to a nuclear test of some sort, and Pyongyang merely shrugs off Washington's sense of "outrage". However, unlike Washington's genuine irritation with Tehran (Iran) there usually seems to be a bit of carrot to go along with the stick aimed at Kim. I keep asking myself why this is the case and recently I found out what may be the reason: oil (!). Off the DPRK East Coast there seems to be a fair bit of deep sea oil which has not been touched, because Pyongyang does not have the technology. Off the West Coast there has been no attempt to develop oil reserves in the North's share of Korea Bay. China has no problems in developing their side of this waterway (and the connecting others), so I do not accept the idea that there is nothing there for the North. Oil deposits do not generally recognise international boundaries! So, how does the US get its energy starved mitts on this oil? Well, we have to have some idea of what is going on in that VERY opaque corner of the world. I have studied it for sometime now (since 1983 actually!) and wish to attach my newsletter comments (well, some of them anyhow!) for your interest:- "I chanced to read, in this morning's Daily Telegraph (London), a really interesting story about the future of North Korea (DPRK) and what various powers seem to be doing about this. A large number of question marks which have been hanging over this 'reclusive Stalinist state' (to use the usual method of the Western press in describing this rather bizarre country) are now, to my way of thinking, being resolved. Have a look at this URL and where I have highlighted in yellow below http://www.telegraph.co.uk/news/worldnews/asia/northkorea/10808719/China-plans-for-North-Korean-regime-collapse-leaked.html .

"China has drawn up detailed contingency plans for the collapse of the North Korean government, suggesting that Beijing has little faith in the longevity of Kim Jong-un's regime. "Documents drawn up by planners from China's People's Liberation Army that were leaked to Japanese media include proposals for detaining key North Korean leaders and the creation of refugee camps on the Chinese side of the frontier in the event of an outbreak of civil unrest in the secretive state. "The report calls for stepping up monitoring of China's 879-mile border with North Korea. "Any senior North Korean military or political leaders who could be the target of either rival factions or another 'military power,' thought to be a reference to the United States, should be given protection, the documents state. "According to Kyodo News, the Chinese report says key North Korean leaders should be detained in special camps where they can be monitored, but also prevented from directing further military operations or taking part in actions that could be damaging to China's national interest. "The report suggests 'foreign forces' could be involved in an incident that leads to the collapse of internal controls in North Korea, resulting to millions of refugees attempting to flee. The only route to safety the vast majority would have would be over the border into China.

"In looking at all of this information, and what I have been following from Chosen Ilbo, The South China Morning Post, and The Japan Times (all of which have good connections, shall we call them, with senior Chinese leaders) we can now probably surmise some quite plausible answers to most of the following questions about the comings and goings in Pyongyang. "1) Why was Kim Jong-un's uncle, Jang Song-Thaek, executed very rapidly after a show trial which was a mockery even by their loose standards? "2) During this 'trial' why was Kim a long way from the danger area in

Pyongyang, apparently inspecting a very remote military base on the DPRK border with China (PRC)? "3) Why has Chosen Ilbo been running, until very recently, a series of articles about possible Korean reunification on its front page? "4) Why was it that US Secretary of State Kerry visited Peking a few weeks ago, with reunification on the docket for detailed talks? "5) Why has the US policy towards DPRK been one of sanctions, but very loosely enforced, when other countries around the world have felt the full weight of Washington's wrath in this regard? The answer to this will be fairly obvious as you read on and think about it. Washington wants a reunified Korea and if a bit of carrot versus sanctions stick is the way to go ... well, why not? "6) Why did Peking (sorry, I still prefer the old spelling!) allow such a sensitive document to be 'leaked' to a Japanese newspaper at a time of fairly intense strain in the relationship between the two countries? "7) Why has the DPRK leadership turned fairly hostile towards its one benefactor, the PRC?

"These are good questions, and if one puts the answers together, I think we can see what lies ahead in Northeast Asia in the foreseeable future. I am not sure that I can answer all of them, but I think I can give you enough on the rest so you can draw some definitive conclusions of your own. Not to forget our old friend the Pi Cycle principle (to emphasise this yet again as it may hold the key for stability throughout the world), we can see that since the Japanese were driven out of their Korean colony at the end of WW 2 (1945) until today have seen nearly 69 years elapse. "The numbers 69 and 2014 are both Pi Cycle numbers and that 2014 is also on Marty Armstrong's War Cycle set of dates. So, my conjecture is, and I have not abandoned this even though the attention of most of the world's media has been focused on Ukraine recently, that Korea is the place to be this year. If there is not going to be a war, then a massive change in how things happen in that area of the world look to be probably imminent. (Well, at least in this year!). This would also fit the possible outcome of a War Cycle change as it would be quite substantial in my view. "Now we can see that the questions (1) and (2) above have a decent answer. In both cases, and I wondered this at the time, it was quite likely that there was a coup either underway in Pyongyang or there was about to be one.

"Kim's uncle, the respected Jang Song-thaek (who many people suspected was really running the show in DPRK with the young Kim Jong-un as some sort of figurehead) simply didn't have the confidence in the Kim bloodlines, especially with a 30 year old at the helm. Kim was made aware of this and had Jang hauled out of the NK Parliament (literally), dragged into a show trial which set records for quickness, and then shot immediately. "Pictures released of Kim after all of this was over showed him looking shocked and stunned at what had happened and what he had had to do. This makes sense if there was a coup about to be undertaken. One does not want to have your potential successor hanging around when the very balance of power was in flux! "Jang was 'convicted' (depending on where one reads the events) of either womanising and/or speculating with, and illegal delivery of, North Korea's plentiful supply of raw materials to Peking. As this seems to have been part of his remit, it seems that his fate was unduly harsh so there was probably something rather more substantial at stake. "If one now looks at Kim's official itinerary at the time of these rather nasty happenings, we see that he was well out of harm's way at a military base on the Chinese border; a rather remote base I understand. If things has gone badly for poor old Kim, then he would have had protection and would not have had far to flee to the relative sanctity of China itself. "Interestingly enough, if one reads the Telegraph article, we see immediately that the entire contingency plan to house fleeing NK leaders and VIPs comes from China! That apparently fits rather well! When Jang had been dispatched and the coup leadership did not have the strength to carry on, only then did Kim return to Pyongyang. In the following weeks, a lot of Jang's followers (read: fellow coup plotters, or a new government-in-waiting) also met Jang's fate. "Now let's look at questions (3) and (4). I watched Kerry's visit to Peking (and reported on it in the newsletter at the time) and I saw precisely nothing! Now clearly Kerry would not make a long visit to China unless he had something to say or wanted to understand the thinking of the Peking leadership. Ultimately, some sort of cover story was released which said zilch in a high sounding manner. "The SK newspapers, which had been fairly excited about reunification – for obvious cultural reasons – stopped their reporting on this. Pyongyang I do not think was pleased with what they were told was happening, as they proceeded to have a lot of 'military exercises' which involved firing off many missiles into the ocean not that far from SK waters. So, the lesson one takes away from this must be that 'something' is being prepared by Peking as far as its long time pain-in-the-neck neighbour is concerned. The question is whether the US was complicit in all of this/would be complicit. "A reader was kind enough to write in and wonder about the Telegraph article. He wondered if a giant quid-pro-quo was in the works whereby PRC would let DPRK collapse and be absorbed into the South. The carry on to this (which would allow the US – through its puppet in SK) would be full access to the Chinese border at the Yalu River. "It would be quite a prize for the US in my view and in turn the US would either allow Taiwan to be reabsorbed into China (a goal of Peking ever since 1949) or else possibly sticking it to the Japanese by recognising PRC claims to all of the oil and mineral resources in the South China Sea. In either event, it would be a win-win and it may be that this reader is well up on his analysis and I commend his thinking along these lines. However, has the US tried a double-cross? Yes, I think they have. "The Telegraph article says that PRC is preparing for the possibility of having millions of NK refugees streaming across the DPRK/PRC border into a portion of China with a goodly number of ethnic Koreans already living there. As I understand it, many of these Koreans are not overly fond of the leadership in Peking and would like to re-join their countrymen in a new sort of Greater Korea somehow. "They are what is called 'restive' in terms which China has used to describe other areas of its vast country: say its far west. Therefore, we can say that Inner Mongolia and NE Manchuria are vulnerable, especially if 5-10 million NK refugees settle there.

"What I think the Peking leadership has come to the conclusion about is that if the US (as per Telegraph) wants to foment something in NK which could cause its collapse, then the State Department has also planned for destablisation of China as a whole by having them absorb a huge number of hungry and desperate people. With China's financial institutions having a tough time right now with many banks having increasingly larger number of bad real estate loans, having ten million desperate Koreans to worry about is not what China wants to see! "The US would love to see all this of course and Peking has probably realised that the entire US plan is lose-lose for them. They are angry in other words and they realise that if the US starts some sort of action which results in the collapse of the Pyongyang Government it will be the Chinese who will have to clean up the mess; and it will be a big one! And what of Pyongyang? What do they think of all of this, especially as they will be front and centre in all of this?

"They know, in my view, and are angry. The NK press has reported that in a visit to the NK's primary military academy for officer training candidates, Kim told a class that they should regard the PRC as their enemy now. This apparently caught the academy's commanders unawares, but they just happened to have the politically correct banners around from the last time (quite some time ago if I remember correctly). "Now why, out of the blue, did Kim make a speech like this? The obvious conclusion is that he is aware of what is happening behind the scenes and is furious. He is being sold down the drain and knows it! "So, what does he do going forward? My guess is that he fires off his fourth nuclear test (however that is configured) and when both PRC and the US are royally annoyed with him he may actually initiate a war with the South which would be ruinous for both halves of the Korean peninsula and, because of the way global economies are interlinked, the damage would reverberate across the world. "Don't forget that SK has the world's 10th biggest economy, and one does simply not remove this from the global economic equations without a lot of really bad things, possibly catastrophic, happening. Is this what the US might wish to see so that some sort of plan could be put into play which might cause widespread disaffection with the Kim regime? It is possible, although to try and calculate how all of this may play out with refugee flows into China is beyond me to be frank.

"And what of today? What can we make (and extrapolate) from all of the news from around the world and how it might all fit? I suspect that Japanese Prime Minister has more than an inkling of NK's impending demise and this may be the reason why he is using every trick in the book to evade the Japanese Constitution's ban of the use of the military abroad. In other words, if the US cannot respond to what Kim is doing with Northern forces, then maybe it can count on Japanese troops, although I think both halves of Korea would be revolted to see the troops from their former colonial overlord back again! "Abe will succeed in my view with his verbal sophistry. The Japanese Constitution allows the use of the military for Japanese security, so Abe is saying that Japanese troops can be used for 'collective security' – other close-by nations together with Japan. He is being painted as a latter day warmonger, but the truth as I see things is a lot deeper than that. "Lastly, we must look at what the US has done to its relationships with PRC. The Chinese appear to distrust Washington and now that they read (and understand through many diplomatic channels I would imagine) how Washington started the whole mess in the Ukraine (see Paul Craig Roberts' massive works on this sorry subject), they wonder if they are being set up to fail. "If they see Russia having trouble in its own backyard, then they must wonder if something similar was planned for them what with perhaps 10 million Korean refugees streaming into NE China. The Communist Government in Peking shares a deep distrust (with other now departed Communist Governments) about instability. They know they have troubles with their banks and vastly overextended balance sheets. They know that banks could easily topple and fail quiet easily and they simply do not trust what Washington may be up to. "It is probably something in this vein which has indicated that Peking and Moscow have agreed to become close friends: they both now realise that they have a common enemy in Washington. How far this friendship will go will probably be seen when President Putin visits Peking later on this month."

This is a fair amount of detail, but there is more – quite a bit actually – but I shall try to keep this down to something which will not bury you in details (well not too deeply in any event!). In order to understand more fully what is going on in DPRK we must look at what the US wants to do globally. As we have been detailing in this book, the search for oil or something which can be used as a substitute (and which is politically acceptable, see comments on Bedini-Schoolgirl; cold fusion etc.) is intense. The US has not been that harsh, when all is said and done, with the regime in Pyongyang and I suspect that the State department has its eye on what I believe are decent sized oil fields on both of DPRK's coasts. That would say a great deal in my view about global oil supplies. The main thing I am looking at is that the US may want a "go-slow" approach to dealing with the Kim Government because it wishes to transfer the 35,000 US troops in South Korea (RoK) to other areas of the world – say the Middle East or possibly to NATO command in Eastern Europe to make a strong statement to Russia's President Putin.

So, how can the US basically emasculate the North from its worries as to how NE Asia progresses? In recent months, there has been strong talk which may point towards some sort of Korean re-unification – that is to say having the North and South get together under one government (Korean and not a colonist regime under one form or another) and to have a reunified Korean Peninsula for the first time in a VERY long time. US Secretary of State Kerry has been making comments to this effect, and there are happenings in the North which indicate that things may be underway to that effect. Predictably, the North is incensed at all of this (and they apparently feel that China/PRC may have sold then out on this issue) and there are two comments from the North Korean official press, Rodong Sinmun on all of this. There is clearly a sense of anger at what the US may (or may not) be doing to DPRK.

In an amazing article in Rodong Sinmun, the gloves came off in describing Barack Obama in a manner which would have done the old Ku Klux Klan proud. Comments about "The Black Monkey" and half breeds not even belonging in a zoo were bandied about. These passed the official censor there, remarkably, and therefore reflect some really pent-up frustration on the part of the senior Party members in Pyongyang. This sort of language is simply not used in any sort official communiqué, even one which goes through the press. The US reply to this was, equally remarkably, moderately restrained. There was the usual condemnation and a sort of "tut-tut, what ARE you people doing" but that was all. No follow on at all and I was looking for it. My best guess is that Washington knows full well the reason for this outburst. Washington and Peking (China) have probably come to an arrangement to finally muzzle the North permanently. They are going to do this, in some manner according the The Telegraph in London (a nice leak!), via a unification of North and South. There have been several articles in leading Southern newspapers (ie Chosen Ilbo) wondering about how the society of the South would be changed by such a merger. So, a merger between the two halves of Korea and a possible merger between the two halves of North America could both be on the cards! What next I wonder?! By the way, here is the jist of the article: amazing: - President Obama a "wicked black monkey" – North Korean state media Korean-only article published by North Korean state media outlet contains highly racist language May 8th, 2014 48 North Korean state media called President Obama a "wicked black monkey" and South Korean President Park Geun-hye an "old prostitute" in a duo of articles and highly inflammatory commentaries published last Friday. The condemnations, which included unprecedented levels of extremely racist and offensive rhetoric, were published following a speech made by President during a visit to South Korea in April and spotted by North Korea watcher Josuha Stanton of the One Free Korea blog, several days after publication. But while an English language article published by the Korea Central News Agency (KCNA) contained just one reference to the terms "monkey" and "prostitute", a separate

Korean language article – published 90 mins later – contained far stronger language, representing previously unseen level of unfiltered racism towards the U.S. President.

INFLAMMATORY LANGUAGE The Korean only article, comprising the direct opinions of four local North Koreans, said Obama resembled a "monkey" and that Park, who hosted him during his recent visit to Seoul, was a "whore". "How Obama looks like makes me disgusted," Kang Hyuk, a worker at the Chollima Ironworks Factory said when translated into English. "As I watch him more closely, I realize that he looks like an African native monkey with a black face, gaunt grey eyes, cavate nostrils, plump mouth and hairy rough ears. "He acts just like a monkey with a red bum irrationally eating everything – not only from the floor but also from trees here and there...Africa's national zoo will be the perfect place for Obama to live with licking bread crumbs thrown by visitors," Kang concluded. Jung Young Guk of the DPRK Ocean Management Office said the timing of Obama's visit – so soon after the sinking of the Sewol ferry – was difficult to understand, adding that Obama had a "disgusting monkey look even though he is wearing a fancy suit like a gentleman". National People's Congress Instructor Choi Yang Sun took offense at the U.S. decision to indefinitely extend the transfer of wartime operational control (OPCON) to South Korea, arguing that President Park had welcomed false promises from Obama by "taking off her underwear". Another citizen quoted in the piece said that South Korean citizens were talking "shit' about Obama "behind his back," pointing out that he was nothing more than a "paper tiger".

Rodong Sinmun also has another story which seems to be based on the reunification idea. As just noted there was a story in the Telegraph of London to this effect, but was couched in a more opaque format of "foreign intervention to destablise the North" which would lead to its collapse. The North was furious when the President of the South picked up on this in a visit to Berlin (how appropriate: to give a Korean unification speech in a country which, until under a generation ago was also divided along political lines!) and we saw the following commentary:- On Park Geun Hye's "Doctrine of Gaining Great Opportunity of Unification" The ghost-like watchword "Gaining a great opportunity of unification" is afloat in south Korea these days. Park Geun Hye is making much fuss about getting ready for "unification" and "forming a preparatory committee for unification", talking about "gaining a great opportunity of unification" whenever a chance presented itself. She also vociferated about the watchword during her trips to neighboring countries and even during her European junket. Philistines and media of her puppet regime are also staging charades about studying the watchword, oft-repeating it. "The doctrine of gaining a great opportunity of unification" is a heinous "doctrine of confrontation of the social systems" and "doctrine of achieving unification of the social systems". It is also a "doctrine of war against the DPRK" and "a doctrine of nuclear disaster". The strange watchword "Gaining a great opportunity" fully reflects the base and ugly nature of philistinism, mammonism that one can lure people with money and it is everything. It is painful and shameful that the country remains divided though nearly 70 years have passed since the partition of the country. It is a vicious mockery and insult to the wishes of the Korean nation for reunification to deny the basic nature of the issue of the reunification of the country and describe it as a bargaining chip for dealers and gamblers. Her doctrine is nothing but the daydream of "achieving unification of the social systems" veiled with the above-said watchword presupposing the "unification under American- style liberal democracy" and the "German-style reunification".

The days of the North now appear to be numbered and it is a question, (always remembering that this year, 2014, is a War Cycle year) which is going to keep Kim Jong-un and his entourage away for many nights I think. Yes, DPRK is what the West might refer to as a "royal-pain-in-the-ass" without question by it seems to me as though it is "being handled". Whether Kim and his regime appreciate what is being done/about to be done or not, I suspect that DPRK's one clear friend, China, may be about to dump them. In a visit of a

North Korean military academy recently Kim made the astonishing speech that "China is now our number one enemy". Hmmm ... with friends like these!

SEGMENT FIVE

CHAPTER THREE

✦✦✦✦✦

THE POPULATION PROBLEM – THERE IS NOT ENOUGH OF US!! GET BREEDING Y'ALL!

Now we must leave the unusual country of North Korea (DPRK) and head towards a more significant story: that of the global population problem. No, this is not what you might think. This is a story of the LACK of people who are apparently NOT clogging our globe and why this unusual circumstance is going to cripple the economies of The West and, by extension, the rest of the world before we are all too much older. Let us commence with the island nation of Singapore, which is where I started to assess what was really happening (following, as is always the case, the money). A couple of years back (it was quite recent actually), I read an article in the Straits Times, which is Singapore's leading paper (well, I think it is anyhow!).

It mentioned that the government there was looking at the population growth of that small island nation (it is about three and a half times the size of the District of Columbia) and did not like what they saw. Yes, there were looking at a rise in population, in line with most of the rest of the world, but it was the wrong type! The Fertility Rate in that nation was a minuscule 0.79. What does this mean, in plain English? It means that women are simply not producing children at anything like the rate which is needed for a strong, economic, and sustainable population. Let's look at this slightly differently. A man and a woman marry and decide to have a few children. In order to be able to replace themselves, these new parents must produce just over two children. The actual number, as far as I can see, is 2.1 children. They have to produce offspring so that when they die, there are two more people to replace them (their children). We allow for accidental deaths and so forth and this is why we arrive at 2 children plus the "0.1" for the accidents. What if, as Zero Population Growth aficionados claim, that if a couple has no children they are doing their part in slowing global population. This is a very superficial way of looking at things as it does not allow for economic considerations and a massive change of population not that many years down the road. The problem of Singapore (and this is true with many other nations around the globe) is that the population they have now pretty well guarantees an economic collapse.

Because Singaporean women do not produce children in anything like the normal replacement rate as held by Fertility Rate theory, the number of elderly people will continue to grow in relationship to the number of people working and producing goods, services, and taxes. With more and more people demanding services for the elderly and the pension payments that go with this, who is going to provide all of the required funds? Confucian tradition demands that the elderly be treated with respect and care, and in Singaporean society this WILL be honoured. But how is this to be done? The planners in Singapore have decided that their population will have to be INcreased, and the only way that this can be done will be to encourage a lot of new immigrants and workers to come to this crowded island nation and work. If the elderly are stopping working because of their advancing years, who are going to replace them at their productive jobs? There are no local candidates in the numbers required and so the immigration barriers are going to come down. The population will be allowed to increase to well over 7 million from the current levels of 6.3 million or so.

This will cause a problem with already high priced housing and so the government is going to continue to reclaim land from the sea and use this to build new apartment blocks and the like for the new arrivals. Yes, there will be (as noted) an increase in population, but so what? When the older Singaporeans start to die off (and they will, along with their co-aged in every in other country across the world) then the population, because of the current imbalances, will start to nosedive. The Zero Population Growth people are going to be able to claim victory and that is fine by me (but please read on!). It reflects the collective decision by Singapore's women not to have children in any quantity whatsoever. If that is what they want, which must mean in extremis the end of Singaporean civilisation, then their wombs have spoken and spoken loudly. However, women are unlikely to do this sort of thing without a solid reason and in numerous articles we are seeing why: the economy. If major corporations are so desperate to squeeze every last penny out of society to feed their already bloated shareholders, then they will doom that society completely. If they are so Hell-bent on keeping wages and benefits as low as possible and keeping taxes equally low to boost their collective bottom lines, there will be consequences. These consequences are that people will not be able to buy any sort of longer lasting home security or even planning for a home, because the economy is too "iffy". Why sign on to a long term mortgage when it is highly likely that you will be laid off or fired from your job (no fault of your own, just corporate greed and indifference) with who knows what results to your home and family? Do you wish to bring a lot of children (or even one or two) into this world when you may not be able to care or raise this child(ren) because of avoidable economic concerns? This is not just me chattering away and causing you to reach for your Dramamine. This what women in Singapore, Japan, and Korea are doing en masse. They do not have the confidence in what lies ahead and so they defer, often for far too long to try later on, having a family. Fertility Rates are low in these three countries and we are going to see the effects of this for sometime to come. Would you like some more proof? Have a look at what I wrote in the newsletter about France recently:-

"There is a template for this population crisis (it is!) and it is to be found, in the main, in today's France. In looking at the ruin of the EU's economy (and that is not just me saying this, just read virtually any comments on the overall mess it is in) we do see that one country – a major one, France – has kept up its Fertility Rate to a hair under the 2.1 replacement levels. "Women there are not afraid to have children as the social benefits are large and continuing. Schools are made easy to enter and in some cases an apartment in Paris (an apparent prized possession in France) can be made available. In other words the economic uncertainties which are seen in so many countries have been ameliorated to such an extent in France that women are willing to have what may still be regarded as a 'traditionally sized family'. The result is that with a steady Fertility Rate, France will not have the problems which are seen in the Far East, North America, and in much of the EU. "The supposed trouble with France is what short-sighted economic publications trumpet over and over again. These periodicals talk about 'punitive tax rates' and 'unwelcome State intervention in the economy'. "Well you asked for all of the problems that are now surfacing with 'rights issues' in the past decade or so, and now that the Fertility Rates are coming home to roost you complain. French bosses are crying at the restrictive laws on the books which make firing people quite difficult. They say that there is no future to investing in France because the tax regime is so bad. The only way, they say, is to invest outside the country in an overseas subsidiary where the margins are good. "They say ... they say, and yet the main Paris stock index, the CAC-40, is up over 55% in the last two and a half years! What a mess they say and yet people think enough of what is happening there to buy French equities for large portfolios! I suspect that the crying and stamping of little French feet is due to the inability of French managers to do as they want compared to what they could do in other countries. "When a French billionaire moved himself and his money to neighbouring Belgium not that long ago, the outcry was deafening. My question at the time was more basic. If France is such a dreadful place to live and invest, how did this man become a billionaire in the first place?"

(End newsletter extract).

So French women are not afraid to conceive and virtually alone in the major industrial countries of the EU, have kept their birth rate at the break-even point of just under 2.1 children per women in their lifespan. So, major industrialists and "Free Marketers" have been complaining in the most derisive terms that the French Government is paying French women to have children and that this is the most intrusive of government policies in general. Well, if French companies and those of The West in general are essentially stopping French women from having children by making the whole process so difficult and uncertain, what do they expect?? Do they expect the French Government to lie down and do nothing while their generally vibrant society slowly withers and dies? The companies therefore have a choice. They can pay high taxes and make laying off expectant parents very difficult and have the French authorities react as they do, OR they can pay decent wages and benefits and encourage women to have children as there is a decent chance that their families will be able to be raised without the excesses of modern capitalism. They cannot have it (the companies that is!) both ways and the proof of this lies in collapsing birth rates globally. However, Western governments in general still specialise in shooting themselves in the economic foot in trying to be all things to all people all the time. Let me now open up (a tiny crack!) the issue of "Women's Rights" in all of this.

For about a generation now we have seen the idea that women, in general, should have equal rights in obtaining managerial positions through the national industrial spectrums. In their efforts to bend over backwards as quickly as possible for all concepts that suddenly rise, governments laid down with breath taking rapidity rules and regulations for women to be treated with extra-special kid gloves. We saw what follows in Japan to a large extent, and we shall return to this benighted nation shortly. What happened? Women had an agonising decision to make; do they have a family or a career which would bring in a lot of extra money into their households? As might be expected they tried to have it all and wound up, exhausted, trying to be a high powered executive as well as a mother. Day care centres (essential in a case such as this I would have thought) became quite prevalent and now cost money which can be not far off what the mother might be making in the workforce herself. So, why do it? The maternal drive is so strong that women simply did not want to give up having children altogether and this was fortified when corporations started to realise that families now had two wage earners and as such had a great deal more spending power. It was also realised that these same families could take a significant financial hit (ie a lay-off because a job was sent overseas). Women, exhausted from "trying to have it all" simply cut back on the number of children they were conceiving. The Fertility Rates suffered accordingly and now governments are saying a collective "Ooops!" and are wondering what they can do. Let us stick with the Asian continent for awhile and look at its major industrial power, Japan. (Well, we can say that this was Japan and now is China, but as I have more data from Japan let's stay there!).

Japan is an island nation, in more ways then one. We used, when I was much younger, to hear the word "inscrutable" used to describe how the Japanese live and work and in my mind this still holds true. The nation is small, land-wise, at something a bit smaller then 60% of the size of Alberta, my home province (which, for my American readers, is slightly smaller than the State of Texas). Into this small-ish land area is squeezed in 125 million people, versus just four million in Alberta. In other words, the big cities in Japan (Tokyo in the main comes to mind) are REALLY big. Greater Tokyo has about 40-45 million people in it, which places it at one of the biggest in the world. Of course, if you live in that giant metropolis, you are living cheek-by-jowl with a lot of other people and are living in small and VERY expensive accommodations. As one may have been aware of, for many decades now, the Japanese economy was the second largest in the world (after that of the United States, of course) and has now slipped into the number three slot after China. It was (and remains, to be honest) a major industrial powerhouse and the stories of the Japanese "Salary-man" putting in 20 hour days was legendary. However, what wasn't asked at that time, was how the wife of such a Japanese employee lived. What did she do in their shoe-box sized apartment, and was this anyway to bring up the next generation? I cannot believe it was, as the Japanese women jumped at the chance to make something of themselves when the American ideals of "Women's Rights" took hold. In Japan, despite this idea, it is still a very much male orientated society and if a woman is trying to advance herself within her company, she must NOT get married or else she will find a very solid glass ceiling over her head. The idea here is that if a woman gets married she may well start to have children and that would distract her from her "all important work" at the company. Therefore, marriages are down, and so are the births of children. The Fertility Rate in Japan is bigger than that of Singapore, but at 1.3-1.4 it is still FAR below the replacement rate of 2.1 as we have discussed. Some months ago, in the excellent British newspaper The Guardian, there was a superb article about Japanese families and why they are not likely to see any sort of increase in the foreseeable future. I wrote a number of newsletter articles on this sorry state of affairs and I wish to reprint them now for your ready reference: -

"In recent letters, I have been assessing the global population levels and found then to be less than satisfactory as regards the economic future of mankind. I have discovered that not too many people agree with me and, as far as I am concerned, that is fine by me! "In short, while population levels are high, most of the 'too high' crowd seems to forget that the internal makeup of various ethnic populations is now tilted towards the aging side. This clearly shows that within a few years we are going to see substantial die offs and consequent reduction of overall national populations. Now, if one considers that if the young (what there are of them!) are anti-pathetic towards breeding on any level, then we should have a situation to gladden the heart of any ZPG advocate!

"Such a situation is now occurring in Japan as we speak. On the just noted article in the British newspaper, The Guardian, a few days ago we see that some 45% of 16-24 year old Japanese women abhor sexual contact of virtually any description. For the men, this works out to about 25%, which is also traditionally high. The implications of all of this are astonishing! What are we to make of this in a population whose Fertility Rate is 1.3 last I saw (and most likely dropping is probably safe to say)? "When one combines that with a central bureaucracy which apparently does not care one jot about all of this, the stage must be set for something catastrophic for Japan. This same bureaucracy also has put out figures showing that by the far off year of 2060, Japan's elderly will be very large relative to the youngsters then. "Given that these numbers were probably complied in 2010 (ie a fifty year window), we see a bureaucracy saying (in effect) that this is a problem which will have to be taken care of in a very distant time. Being a practical person myself, I merely note that last year the sales of Japanese adult diapers exceeded those for infants for the first time. That is what you should be considering in my view!

"The story is about four days old and comes under the heading of Japanese shunning sex. I strongly suggest you find and read it: long but worth it! I spoke to someone I know who made the acid comment that we can forget the fifty year projections noted above. "The damage to Japan will have been done in ten years, and possibly as little as five (given that trends are usually very tough to reverse, especially one such as this). The bottom line must be that if women do not wish to have children born into the nation into which they are such an integral part, then that nation dies. It is rather simple!

"My own particular beliefs are that we can chose the body and the nation into which we incarnate (subject to ones personal karmic balances). Therefore, Japanese women being born into Japan now apparently feel no compunction in keeping the population on an even keel in their chosen homeland. In other words, they are Japanese by choice but feel no burning desire to keep Japan going by breeding the next generation. "Well, if women will not perform and with the traditional Japanese reticence at allowing large scale immigration not having been reduced to any extent, Japan looks like a doomed society, and probably a lot sooner than most people expect. In the Guardian article we see many reasons trotted out as to why children are not be born into that country.

"Basically, they revolve around having good jobs and not willing to have a boss fire them (in theory as opposed to practice) because they became married - with a probable pregnancy to follow at some point. The other reason is one which is going to be much more difficult to fight: cultural exhaustion. In the article one sees this exhaustion mentioned several times. With endless problems in trying to raise a household and the children which invariably accompany such an enterprise, the effort required is apparently deemed not to be worth it. "It is too much investment of emotion and for little return. The cost of living is very high and Japanese women do not feel like having to work at a glass-ceilinged job and then return home to looking after their residence. The person I spoke to, which I mentioned earlier, made me aware of another possibility: Fukushima.

"I have written regarding this nuclear atrocity which is now well over three years old and not only shows no sign of being resolved but actually may even be getting a great deal worse. No less an American political authority such as Paul Craig Roberts feels that the radiation from the crippled nuclear reactor has by now seeped into the ground waters which provide the drinking waters for metropolitan Tokyo, and then when all is said and done, some 50 million people may be at risk. "I would imagine that there are many such stories circulating in that area of Japan and so what is a young woman to think? The simple reply is that it is not worth the trouble of raising a family: that Japanese society has played itself out and that there is no point in even trying to be a heroine and buck a clear trend.

"This not just Gerry Agnew making wild comments. In the last five years Japan's population has declined in each year from 130 million to 126 million. So, in this environment, where are the nation's leaders? Where is Prime Minister Abe and his very voluble Deputy Prime Minister? What are they saying and doing? "Well, Abe seems to be interested in worshipping Japan's military ancestors (and infuriating his Korean and Chinese neighbours) at the Yasukuni Shrine, and his deputy has more than once called on simple elimination of the tube people (his term for older Japanese who are in nursing homes and riddled with feeding tubes and so forth to keep them alive).

"I suppose that is one way of looking at things as it WOULD free up quite a few younger Japanese workers from taking care of the elderly and make them available for more profitable, export-led jobs. He assumes that once a worker stops intubating the elderly that this worker will quickly shift over to loading export ships and so forth. Not too bright that assumption I think! "Perhaps 25-40% of workers could be retrained for such work, and then what about the rest? We can also go a step further and wonder about the upcoming flood of retirees from the Post-War generation. Will the Abe government want to kill them all as well? However, the die has now been cast here. "I am willing to bet that as more and more Japanese jobs become open because of retirement and possible emigration to the United States under the new immigration initiative there which we have been discussing recently in these pages, we shall start to see, in the leading Japanese newspapers, a call for a cull of the elderly (euthanasia in other words). This would save the Japanese Treasury a LOT of money and have distressed pension funds jumping for joy.

"And what of less extreme measures? Abe has been trumpeting new day care centre initiatives and new deals for working women, to which I merely wonder just what token measures (given Japanese society) will be announced. Remember that it will be the women of Japan who will be the final arbiters of such attempts to write solutions to something which may be completely insoluble. As an economist, I simply wonder just how Abe is going to find the money to afford anything like such programmes which have proven to be so expensive elsewhere in the world. Let us have a look-see at what Capitalism and Socialism have to say about such things.

"Initially, we can look at France, which is being pilloried by just about everybody for daring to have the effrontery to show the world a GDP which is comprised of about 57% of government spending. The same articles also tell us that most major French companies now have about 90% of their sales overseas and that this is the norm in France where it makes no real sense to carry on business. Things have got to change there is the unspoken word, but is this correct given the window on which we are looking at here - that is to say population growth?

"I think not! If we look at the "liberated" world of unbridled capitalism we see Fertility Rates of 1.2 in Korea, 1.3 (estimated in wretched Japan), the EU in the 1.4/1.50 area or so, and in the US we see 1.50/1.60 in the all important white population (which I have been told is key to this nation's problems) and so on and so forth. What this said was that greedy corporate bosses (to quote so many columnists) are grabbing all they can for short term benefits because, as we all know, the future is always some distance off and never something to be concerned about. Not this time!

"Now we come to France and its 'silly' system of internal free spending by the central government. Here we see (and I had to check this twice to make sure it is correct) a Fertility Rate of right around 2.1 (!). In other words, while most other spendthrift nations are looking at disaster not that far down the road, France can look forward to the future with confidence. "Yes, there is always the problem of emigration to other EU countries, but on balance, France with its free spending is fine! What all this says (and it is fairly easy to corroborate) is that France spends a lot of money on children and families. This seems to be a hangover from the 1870/71 Franco-Prussian War when it was held that the reason why France lost was that it simply did not have enough population to be able to stem the Germanic hoards. This hit such a nerve that even today France is always frightened of not being able to have enough people to stem some future disaster. After this brief re-visit to France, let us return to Japan and North America for a quick look-see.

"In the Guardian article noted before, we saw a comment to the effect from one of the females being interviewed about what Abe was trying to do with day care centres and so forth. She was not that impressed and said that the burden of proof was on the Abe Government. She would not, in other words, willingly give up her exciting and well paying job to retire to home life and start breeding for Japan. "There is the trust issue to be sure (as noted before) as the feeling that 'Japan is past it' is going to be hard to dispel. A government which is as right-wing as that of Mr. Abe is going to leave the impression that it will do as little as possible to reverse the brewing Japanese catastrophe. This is also (no kidding!) unhelpful as well. If we now return to France, we see that French women are quite confident that many social programmes which are very family friendly are not going to be reversed anytime soon, and as such it is probably quite safe to conceive several children (France pays on a sliding scale apparently).

"So, France will be around for a long time to come whereas many other nations cannot even begin to say the same. Aha! You might say. What about the US with its huge, pending, immigration bill? Can't nations import skilled workers en masse (to stick with French idioms here!) as required? "Isn't that what the US and Canada are doing right now with all sorts of bonuses for people coming to Alberta? No, this is a short term solution for a long term problem. Essentially beggaring thy neighbour cannot work for whatever you make with your new workers cannot readily be sold overseas. How can it, apart from niche markets here and there? If you purloin workers from overseas and hence weaken those economies, who is going to buy your nice shiny new cars and glitzy gimmicks? "At best you will see your sales either stagnate or decline, and then what has been gained? However, the US is going to go ahead with this plan and will gain a few years before hard-pressed CEOs go running to Washington looking for new handouts. I think the scorecard must read: Socialism 1, Capitalism 0.

"Ok, I can hear you say, so what? So what if a bunch of undersexed Japanese men prefer to drink sake and watch scantily clad maidens in porn or anime movies as a proxy for the real thing? The trouble is that there are (in this wretched financial global economy) going to be a lot of knock-on effects. "If we take the example of Japanese Government Bonds (JGBs) what happens to the popular ten year maturities if some learned papers are put out by Goldman Sachs or Bank of Tokyo decrying what is happening and wondering just how

Japan will be able to finance or repay existing bonds as they become due. "True, we are not going to see substantial reductions in the Japanese population overnight, but if potential investors are warned that within a generation there are going to be problems along these lines, then interest coupons on either existing or to be issued JGBs will be jacked up, possibly sharply with the prospects of a severe recession (combined with a falling number of young people available to do the jobs which will still need skilled workers).

"This will ripple around the world and it will not be one which can be rectified by a simple change of money supply issuance, because there is a fundamental reason why this recession is happening. Yes even in America with tens of millions of immigrants coming to its shores to fight fertility problems, may see a lack of jobs for all of these poor souls who may then simply turn tail and go home - probably to rapturous welcomes given their highly in-demand skill sets! "Nevertheless, we are looking at a real recession problem not that many years down the road (and to reiterate this will not be a recession caused by tangled money supplies and over-valued exchange rates - it will be a REAL recession caused by collapsing markets globally) and bonds have a tendency to discount this sort of bad news. I see nothing but bad news here, sad to say!

"So, let's sum up this probably over-long article. Japanese women seem to be most unwilling to perform the major function of women: to guarantee the continuance of Japanese society, by having babies. If this refusal continues (and there is no indication that it will change) then Japan is finished as the nation we know today. Sorry, that's just the way it is. "Japanese women have apparently given up, caught between the cost of living, cost of housing in particular, and relationships which are not all that might be promised. They wonder why it is that their country has not already collapsed what with the probable lies surrounding Fukushima, and with who knows what else waiting in the wings. "In their hearts, they probably wonder why it is that their Prime Minister worships the past glories of the Japanese military and cannot see why he does not know what is changing in his country; and changing so rapidly. They probably even wonder if there will be a call for elder Japanese to be euthanised and then what?

"The Japanese seem to have a death wish in their popular culture as represented by anime. In three such movies I have seen, Japan is either wiped out (Vexille) completely or comes perilously close in the Appleseed series. Even in the 1995 classic 'Blue Seed', Japan is on the verge of being turned into a nation of plants only to be saved at the last minute. What is with all of this cultural flagellation anyhow? If these films truly represent the inner feelings of Japan, then I cannot see any way for Japan to avoid completing its ritualistic suicide with women simply closing their wombs". (End a very long series of quotes from my newsletters).

We should write a bit more on this, both on behalf of Japan and also South Korea. What do their women want anyway? I do not believe that Japanese women want to even try to raise a family in an urban mess such as Tokyo, or Nagoya, or Osaka, or ... (fill in the blank). They are basically, as I read what they are thinking and doing, considering themselves only as baby machines with nothing for themselves. This would be carried on even to the extent of having a normal husband and wife relationship with husbands having to spend more and more time away from their homes and families because of ever increasing corporate demands on their time. Japanese women, apparently, have no desire to spend their lives in such a manner. The current Japanese Government of Mr. Abe is now completely the wrong thing at the wrong time. His main wish is to throw women a bone (so to speak) as regards having children so that he can resume what is going to be one of the most conservative Japanese administrations in quite some time. Let us see if what he wants makes sense in the current environment of falling numbers of workers to handle major goods producing jobs. He wants to revise the Japanese Post-War Constitution so that Japan can start to intervene overseas again! Yes, this is couched in the most harmless of terms but it seems to this observer that the hand of Washington's State Department can be detected here! Washington (despite all sorts of noises about "pivoting to Asia") really wants to try and corner Russia and to thereby defang Iran and make what is left of the Middle East oil fields as safe for US interests as can be. This means that Washington needs a reliable ally in East Asia to keep watch on North Korea and, to a much lesser extent, on China itself. So, Mr. Abe, with a looming demographics crisis of unimaginable proportions, seems willing to commit possibly large numbers of young Japanese men to this refurbished military! This is insane, and one wonders just what pressures he has been put under to do this? What is the quid-pro-quo? In South Korea, this situation is even more desperate. The Fertility Rate there is down to about 1.3 but this is well up from the 0.98 we saw not that many years ago. By the way the Koreans have congratulated themselves on this fairly rapid turnaround, but whatever they are saying publicly they must still be having severe doubts internally in private conversations. They are nowhere close to "break-even" shall we call it, and in the major newspapers they are only starting to come to grips with the underlying cause of the problem.

This revolves around, predictably enough after looking at Japan, problems with women finding suitable men, finding reasonably priced housing, and in Korea very high school fees which make having even one child problematical. As is with the case with Tokyo, the Korean capital of Seoul now is home to close to 20% of the entire South Korean population. In a country with only a small amount of land area, the Koreans have crammed into Seoul over 10 million people, making it the fifth largest city in the world. How can one cope with a declining Fertility Rate when the overriding national objective of government after government there is economic and financial growth? Do they not realise the danger they are in? I believe they do, but they have no way to rectify this without what so many bureaucrats would call "starting a national panic". What I suspect is going on is what Washington is probably angling for in the entire region: merging the two Koreas as we have discussed previously. With North Korea effectively removed from many contentious issues with such an event, the South could also breathe easier knowing that North Korean men, looking at incredibly luxurious housing in the South (by their standards), would find it quite easy to have families very probably started by some sort of "relocation allowance" funded by various Southern reunification funds which are known to exist. Again, we should refer back to the reunification of the two Germanys at the end of the 1980s/early 1990, to see what happened.

A "Solidarity Tax" was passed in the old West Germany to fund a great deal of the individual expenses associated with the reunification and there is no reason to suppose that this would not happen today half a world away in Korea. It is all very expensive to be sure, but Washington gets what it wants (which, in the final analysis, is the most important aspect of all of this) and the South, in terms of bigger families and more working age men suddenly coming into the Southern workforce, would get its desires met as well. Bit of a tough blow for the North's Kim though! However, in my view, the reunification would be nothing more than a short term palliative. When all was said and done, the problems of finding more and more workers to fill empty Southern jobs and to give enough slack in the overall economy for renewed growth would probably "be handled". However, without additional longer term ways of getting Koreans to produce more babies to offset a huge die off over the next few decades, it will all probably be for naught.

And what about the US, Canada, and the EU countries? What do they do as they have (except for France) the same problems as Asia? The culture is somewhat different here. Canada ran a series of ads on television last year saying that Canada needed a lot of foreign workers because it was losing something like 1,000 skilled workers every day because of the baby-boom finally becoming old enough to retire. Easy-to-obtain visas let a LOT of foreign workers into the country, but the visas were not properly issued and instead of having many skilled workers taking jobs (ie in the Tar Sands) where they were needed, unscrupulous managers hired many workers to do the so-called menial, low paying, jobs which clearly was not intended. This is being rectified as I write these lines and probably no long term damage to the Canadian labour structure will have been done ultimately. What struck my eye was that the federal agencies in Ottawa were willing to act very quickly to counteract what was thought (and is, clearly) to be a serious loss of highly skilled workers. They did not react as did their Japanese and Korean counterparts and simply say that "we are going to have problems over the next 40-50 years so there is not much that can be done now". They assumed that there was an imminent crisis and reacted. The fact that they reacted without enough thought is a different matter entirely.

The USA is using a different approach altogether. What has been done in the past was to open the floodgates for "the world's poor and dispossessed" and to use the idea of a "Melting Pot" so that new immigrants, no matter where they came from, would be welcome and would combine their skills with existing Americans for the betterment of the country as a whole. Today we see a huge immigration bill slowly wending its way through Congress and I suspect that Congress will probably give US businesses all they could dream of: skilled workers who will work for sub-par wages and hence increase corporate profits again and again. If this means that underschooled and unskilled US workers are effectively thrown on the scrapheap, well so be it! The numbers of workers coming to America will be staggering. Some estimates I have seen, when one takes into account the families of immigrants, could boost the US population by 100% over the next 20-30 years from 320 million to nearly 2/3 of a billion! That's a lot of people by any stretch and I wonder where they will all go and what sorts of resources they will consume as they start their version of "The American Dream". In looking at the US, we should consider also what leading political figures are doing about all of this and how it is likely to play out as time progresses. From what I have been able to find out, it seems that the US Fertility Rate among the white population is something like 1.5 or so. Adding in the very prolific Mexicans, it jumps up to perhaps 1.80-1.90; or not that far short of break-even at 2.1. What is Hillary Clinton doing about all of this, and what does she probably feel about the whole thing? To answer this reasonably, we go back to the speech she gave in Los Angeles in November 2013 which was given to an overflow crowd of Spanish speaking Los Angeles residents. Put simply, Latinos love her and will deliver their votes to her in overwhelming numbers. If Hillary can get through Congress (and my betting is that she will given the monumental short-sightedness of US businesses) the immigration bill which has been talked about endlessly in the US press, then we shall see immense numbers of Mexicans come north.

Why is this? Hillary said that NAFTA (the free trade agreement binding Canada, US, and Mexico into an economic grouping) should be expanded through closer and closer relationships between the three NAFTA nations. It is clear, and I shall bet that the Republican leadership in Congress knows this better than anyone, that she wants to open the doors to skilled Mexican workers to come north. Already we are seeing that deportations of Mexicans without the proper visas is diminishing. Mexicans who should be on their way back home are staying in other words. If they stay and are "legalised", with many of their friends and family now being invited to come to the US, we shall see many grateful Mexicans who will be thanking Hillary at the ballot box in 2024. The sheer numbers here may very well, with an overwhelming majority, swing the election decisively to Hillary. Well, doesn't the GOP know this? Why are they doing what they are doing, which is to get the immigration bill passed? This party is trapped by the desires of their supposed base – big business – to get cheap workers into the United States literally NOW so that wage bills can be cut back as soon as possible and profits can resume an uninterrupted flow upwards. The big thing here is that new workers may not know that much about what are called "fringe benefits" in the US and with health care costs literally exploding, the costs to the big corporations are becoming most uncomfortable.

So, for them, do we see lower wages and fewer fringe benefits?! What's not to like? So, Speaker Boehner and the rest of the GOP bigwigs are caught trying to play politics while they are going to get trampled by Mexican workers coming north to vote for Hillary because she is perceived to be friendly to the aspirations of Mexican workers. What's a poor Republican to do anyway? Nothing, is the clear answer except to watch the future of your party simply disappear. (Perhaps this is another reason to get Texas Senator Ted Cruz on the ballot come November 2024, despite the clear handicap of his being born in Canada – a Constitutional no-no, or at least it is supposed to be). Finally, on this question of population and a lack of skilled workers, what can we learn from the EU - excluding France? In reading about the troubles in Germany (and this country, built on exports after WW 2) one wonders if the Europeans have any clue. In Germany, the noted German newspaper Der Spiegel, ran a couple of articles a year or so ago on a growing shortage of workers in Southern Germany. It seems that firms there, in the German industrial heartland, are short of something like 5 million workers but do NOT like the idea of filling out massive numbers of government forms to get the required workers on board. There is also the question of having to train the new workers to speak German which apparently is time consuming (read expensive; can't have that now can we?!). All of which makes no sense. Why is this? Well, Germany is part of the EU and hence can import workers from all over Europe as required, whether they speak German or not. In fact, there are German classes for new arrivals on an ongoing basis! What all this tells me is that there is an unhealthy streak of xenophobia in Germany, even to this day.

And what about places such as Italy, Spain, and Portugal which also use the single currency Euro? How are they doing and what is their outlook? Basically they vary between terrible and ghastly (define those terms as you will, they are both Bad with a capital "B"). In Italy we see persistent high unemployment and the employment system, which has served Italy so well since the end of WW 2, seems to be under threat. This system revolved around the concept of a "guaranteed job" which might sound "socialistic" to an American but worked very well over there. Now some of the high-brow EU leaders think that youngsters should quit these jobs and "see what you can find and what you can make of yourselves". Really? With very high unemployment, people are going to start quitting their jobs?? All this so Italian companies can shed "excess" labour to be "more competitive". The divide between management and shop floor people is as wide as ever, and this is with the population problems Italy currently suffers under. The fertility rate there is far below the critical 2.1 level. Population, for some years now, has been falling to boot. The country never seems to have been able to adjust to the single currency Euro as the Government in Rome had always devalued the old Lira whenever things "needed to get done".

This is no longer possible, for obvious reasons, and it does not look like the economy is going to recover to any great extent when Germany is doing moderately well. There has generally been a divide between North and South Europe for decades, if not centuries, and there is no indication that this will become any better. In fact, with Germany needing skilled workers and the US immigration system looking to vacuum up just about anything that moves in the next decade or so, how can things get better for Italy and Southern Europe in general? It can't is probably the most reasonable answer. Elsewhere in what is fashionable (but, of course, politically incorrect) to call the backward parts of the EU, we see Spain and Portugal. Both countries joined the Euro thinking that it would be so good for their economies to have a bit of internal German-style discipline, but this has not been the case. In the case of Spain we see sky-high unemployment at something like 27% with youth jobless at perhaps twice this level. Just imagine what the headlines would be if we saw numbers like this in the US! So far the Spaniards have suffered in silence, and I suspect that many of the brighter and more skilled workers will be making tracks for the US after the immigration bill there becomes law. Why not? Given the huge numbers of Mexicans already in the US with many more to come (with Hillary pushing the gates open herself!) there would not be a language barrier to any great extent. Additionally, with many nations in Central and South American having Spanish as a first language (who says colonial rule doesn't have long term benefits?), there is plenty of opportunity elsewhere. Spain is not going to have an easy time it seems to this observer! Again, for your own contemplation, with a fertility Rate of 1.5, how CAN Spain recuperate?

Lastly, we look at little Portugal. Why bother with this minor flyspeck on the EU scene you may ask? Well, the leader of the EU comes from there and it is another example of a country at the periphery of this vast trading bloc being left to twist in the wind. (One wonders what the Ukraine and the other Eastern European nations are going to do, over time, when they all subject to the EU monetary prison which is the Euro!). And what does poor little Portugal (which has been desperately poor for so much of its history) do to try and alleviate unemployment which is not as bad as Spain's but "bad enough" shall we say? Again, we go to its history and see that there were nations in Africa which were colonised by Portugal in the frenzy by Europe, in days gone by, to grab what others possessed come what may. I look at the country of Angola which is Portuguese speaking and which is immensely rich because of its oil deposits. True, it is ruled by what many regard to be a despotic form of government, but no one wants to rock a very rich boat! Portuguese citizens go there and set up shop with all sorts of ideas; a lot of them being in the electronic communication industry. It is not hard to get a visa to go there for many years, and make money. Clearly this cannot be done back home in Portugal in the present state of circumstances! In a study done by the major German newspaper, der Spiegel, last year we saw that the Angolan economy in the period 2000-2013 grew a total of over 230%. I would imagine that the rulers of that nation cannot be displeased at what they are seeing, although the gap between the newly rich and the rural poverty is immense. Nevertheless, how can any nation – especially one like Portugal – allow entrepreneurial types to simply leave taking their money and skills with them? How can Portugal, with a Fertility Rate of 1.5 do this for any decent period of time and apparently not realise the danger they are putting themselves in? Well, let's wrap up this section on population shall we? How is it that global population experts can say (apparently endlessly) that the world is over- populated and yet I can write for as long as I have on the serious problems faced by the so-called "Advanced Nations" and their population imbalances?

How, you may well ask, can we reconcile these seemingly disparate viewpoints? This is politically incorrect (what follows) but I have to write it in any event. If we take a country like Niger (an impoverished wreck of a nation in Central Africa) we see the Fertility Rate at something over 7. Yes, I would imagine that many of these children perish in infancy given the primitive conditions into which they are born, but this is the sort of place where much of the world's population comes into existence. In a much larger nation (population-wise) such as Nigeria, we see this key measurement at 5.3. It is estimated, as the relatively pampered population of The West sees a continuous decline over the next half century or so, we could see maybe half a billion Nigerians – all things being equal. This is the crux of the problem. Vast numbers of human beings are classified as "useless" because they have no skills which are recognised as being worth anything in terms of the money/economy driven West. Effectively, the feeling is, what good are people who spend short lives grubbing around in the dirt and have no idea what a computer hard drive is? What good is an illiterate African (or Indian from one of the lower casts) as someone who cannot build a house or dissect a balance sheet? Why do countries such as Italy stop hoards of luckless would-be immigrants from Africa from coming there, even though the Italian population situation is such that additional people to do various menial jobs should be in demand? One of the great sentiments from the US Revolutionary War period (and perhaps one of the most profound ever) was "All men are created equal". Until very recently it was the shining light in US society and certainly was the guiding force for the US Civil Rights era. In today's world, with its unremitting focus on money, power, and a clearly unsupportable idea that economic growth can be unstoppable, this idea of the ages is sadly no more.

Looking at Germany (above) with its latent xenophobia, and Italy (even though it needs the people) turning away African economic immigrants by the boatload, I wonder what these nations are thinking as a collective. With a falling population (in the case of Italy) and a weak Fertility Rate, do they really want to cease to exist as a viable nation a generation or so down the road? Why do they bury their heads on this? (Well, I'm sure we know the answer: no black Africans allowed here as they are inferior). There! I have said it and I challenge you to prove me wrong. In the case of Japan (to take one final example) public opinion polls say, by a large margin, that the Japanese do NOT want large scale immigration at all! Bye-bye, Japan: do the math. In all of this intellectual tussle, we keep coming back to (I suppose, here)

President H. Clinton and her open door policy to fellow NAFTA member, Mexico. It will happen if she wins; bank on it! The United States will scour the globe looking for potential immigrants to come to "The Land of the Free". In some articles I have read, these would-be immigrants do not even have to bring their skills, if they have any. The immigration bill, in one of its editions, allows for something that the US has not encouraged for many decades now: unskilled immigrants. What a damning blow to the tens of millions of Americans who do not have a job or who do not have elementary skills to even seek one! Yet, if the US starts to hoover up all of the reasonable looking immigrants, what happens to Japan, Italy, Germany, Portugal, Spain, and one can clearly go on and on? There will be two classes of people in the world: those who have skills and can go anywhere and those who have little to offer and will left alone to breed and consume. Until the baby-boomers start to die off in large numbers (which, obviously, must happen) global population will continue to grow.

All men will continue NOT to be created equal! The remarkable thing about this horrible attitude is that it is so wrong! Old stereotypes die so hard it seems. Consider modern Africa if you would. The excellent German newspaper Der Spiegel (yes, I do read others but this one always seems to have cutting edge analysis) did a piece on Africa recently. Far from being a continent full of head hunters and disease, with possibly prehistoric animals in its trackless swamps, in many countries (thirteen I count) there are more cell phone contracts per 100 people than there are in the USA! A good comment I read dealt with an entrepreneur who had set up his own company and was working on a way to bring cell technology to really back-of-beyond villages. These villagers would then use their cell phones to do rudimentary banking! This is amazing and one wonders about countries such as Italy which seemingly have no interest in "backward Africans". Their country is slowly falling apart (population and Fertility Rate-wise) and they turn their backs on geniuses such as these? Perhaps there is a turning point in European history where European states fade into history, and we might be living in it now. Perhaps I shouldn't pick on Italy as I am sure that many other

European nations are probably seeing the same sort of attitude in their domestic populations. Fine, they shall all share the same fate.

Well, I have written my piece on population problems and how they are likely to be resolved. This always assumes that there is not some bloody, God-awful, war which eats up millions of young lives (women this time as well, sadly) which will exacerbate the shortage of what we might call "Fertility Rate Workers" even more. (Question which just occurred to me: Does the US want the unskilled workers in the immigration bill to be able to join the military and so preserve the precious skilled workers?).

However, for Americans as a whole (and this is ESPECIALLY true with the enormous quantities of baby-boomers either retired or about to be retired) what happens to their pensions? What happens with Social Security, which supposedly has the vast resources to pay the "Boomers" off for many years, given longevity rates these days? Can it survive with perhaps two or three workers to pay the benefits of one retiree? And this subject must go hand-in-glove with the analysis of badly skewed populations in much of the world – as we have just discussed. Tens of millions of baby-boomers are going to retire and want pensions; ideally commensurate with the salaries they received just before they retired. This cannot possibly happen as we shall now see in the last chapter of this book. It will not be pleasant reading but for those who have stuck with me for all of this time, I urge you in no uncertain terms to read this.

SEGMENT SIX

CHAPTER ONE

✦ ✦✦✦✦ ✦

HYDRO-ELECTRICITY – YES, THIS IS A DECENT RENEWABLE (YEAH! THEY FINALLY FOUND ONE THAT WORKS??)

So, Solar Power and Wind Power either do not work or else need a lot of further research; to be kind about it. What other sources do our intellectual betters have in mind anyway? There are all sorts of wondrous things which have been trotted out, but what do they really do in the final analysis, with one possible exception which looks like being torpedoed by (what else?) political concerns.

We have biomass, tidal power, natural gas (now a favourite of Mr. Pickens), geothermal power, and hydro-electric power. The latter has been around for many years now and comprises a lot of electricity for power hungry North America (read the United States and, in particular, the Northeastern US). However, to deal with "hydro" first, there are problems brewing and these tie in directly with "The Merger" we mentioned earlier on in the book.

Hydro electricity is formed, basically, when man dams a large, fast flowing river, and uses the action of the water to spin turbines which, in turn, generate a lot of electricity. The giant rivers of Northern Quebec and in Labrador (part of the Canadian province of Newfoundland for those who may have doubts) send vast amounts of this precious resource, via giant power pylons (and these really are huge, I have seen them), to the US markets. There are two difficulties to be overcome here, and I do not believe that either has been really addressed.

First is that these giant dams have an average lifespan of about fifty years. I remember in the middle 1970s both Quebec and Labrador were caught up in the midst of a terrific building boom (I worked in the bank branch which did all of the financial transfers for the major Labrador projects, and they were massive). We are now not far from the fifty year time line and I have seen precious little which tells me that neither the Newfoundland nor Quebec Governments have set aside cash reserves to repair/restore these dams or even try to build new projects.

It seems that both Governments are simply content to rake in the hydro cash, in one form or another, and spend it as fast as possible. They have fallen into the easy trap of thinking that these flows of funds will continue as long as the water flows continue to spin the turbines and that will be (of course) "forever". The "hydro dividends" are now a structural part of spending programmes for these two governments and it could be very difficult to disengage from such receipts and to actually spend money in rectifying any potential time problems for the existing dam structure.

Well, something will have to be done. We can also say that the current series of dams tend to let accumulate naturally occurring dirt from river flows (aka "silt") which will, over time, clog intake pipes and so forth which will, at the very least, reduce the output of critically needed hydro power. It may be that the relevant hydro corporations spend time and money removing the silt, but it is not something which one hears about. One also does not hear, apart from very irritated Indian tribes (or Native Americans if you prefer) that the flow of fish is also reduced which many of these local tribes need to live on as have their ancestors for thousands of years. It is probable, sorry to say, that this lifestyle is to be freely sacrificed so that the unending demand for hydro power can continue to be supplied without significant interruption to the industrial estates in the US Northeast.

I feel fairly confident in writing this as in my home province of

Alberta there is much controversy about the toxic runoff from the Tar Sands reaching Lake Athabasca and causing severe distress to the Indian/First Nations communities around the remote town of Fort Chipewyan in Northern Alberta. What I suspect will happen is two fold. In the 1970s, the imaginative Premier of Quebec Robert Bourassa (nicknamed "Bob le Job" for his unusual means of hydro development which would promote Quebec employment) was actually considering building a 100+ mile dam across the mouth of James Bay, which lies at the bottom end of Hudson Bay. The idea was that the massive flow of water between the two bays would generate unimaginable amounts of hydro power, most probably for export to the US. The financing would have been daunting, estimated at something like $ 100 billion dollars which would have been a formidable amount to raise in the post 1974 financially scarred landscape. The technical problems where also cited as being "insurmountable" which is politician speak for "don't even try this and risk humiliating me!". The plan went nowhere, needless to say.

What I want to mention now is the second of the two points noted above. What happens to all of this if "The Merger" between Canada and the United States which I have written about previously, goes ahead? The US has unlimited amounts of the world's reserve currency (ie the US$) and can finance anything it wants on this continent. If the technology was not available in 1975 or so (ie the James/Hudson Bay project), would it be available today?

With the enormous advances in computer science and engineering since then, I am willing to bet that it would be. Certainly, the geographical imperatives surrounding the US economy these days (ie the acute demand for water if nothing else) would make some sort of effort mandatory on the part of the newly merged governments of Canada and the United States.

Economic growth, the mantra of US industry, would demand new and more powerful energy sources. Besides damming the great rivers of Northern Canada for more hydro power, the James/Hudson

Bay project would be irresistibly attractive. It is quite possible, again in my opinion, that the prime movers and shakers who really run the US economy might have had this project (among others I hasten to add as I trust I made clear in my earlier chapters on this subject) in mind when they started their "Merger" project. Time will tell, but economic imperatives cannot be ignored on this scale!

SEGMENT SIX

CHAPTER TWO

✦✦✦✦✦✦

BIOMASS – LET'S BURN OUR WAY
TO ENERGY INDEPENDENCE!

So, there is a lot of interest in Northern Canada as far as I can see here. This and the Alberta Tar Sands (see many comments from before) will keep merger talks alive and well, of that I am sure. However, while a merger within North America would satisfy a lot of queries about "how do we manage", there must be other possibilities. Solar and Wind Power I am justifiably sceptical on, so what do we look at next?

There are minor things right now such as "Biomass". This is a fancy way of saying "burning wood chips, logs, and basically anything which grows and is combustible". The sellers of this idea tell us of the wonderful ways that we can use this. We can thin out forests which are clogged with all sorts of undergrowth and which are very prone to fires. If one looks at the wildfires which very often burn out of control in dry states such as California, we see that they start and expand rapidly because of excessive undergrowth.

In assessing this further, we see many ecologists who do not want to see Mother Nature "hurt" in some manner (such "hurting" being critical to Mother Nature's managing vast areas of forests). It must be clear therefore they have little idea what they were "protecting". The undergrowth has to be cleared, and if man will not allow this to happen, then there are more extreme ways – fires – of getting it done. What irritates me about this method of providing energy (through controlled burns which can heat water and turn turbines and the like) is that what one group of ecologists want to have happen is often bitterly opposed by others. Speaking personally, I have never understood biomass and its appeal. Surely we can run out of forests long before the real shortages of energy/electricity have been addressed and I am allowing for the "managed forest" theory which holds that we can plant forests and nurture them to grow and expand to meet production quotas and goals.

Sorry, but Nature doesn't work like that! Go and find a forest somewhere and walk in it, and then have a good look see and how Nature has put it together. Nature puts different kinds of trees all in the same general area and at different spacings and so forth. In today's planned forest we see the same kind of tree (the kind which brings the maximum profit to a logging company) planted a few feet apart in perfect rows. So what, you may ask? Simply this; what happens if disease breaks out in the trees planted by man through his forest companies? The trees are not separated by other types of different trees, so the disease or insect infestation will roar through the single growth forest at an incredible rate. The infected trees will then be good for little if anything! If there are a dozen different types of trees in a natural forest, then it is a fair bet that the disease may not spread as fast or at all.

If we do get a disease in a real forest, it may even be slow enough to be treated by the forest company concerned. We can also wonder about forest creatures as well as the trees. A forest is composed of trees of all sorts as well as an amazing number of different animals, all of which interact with the trees and plants which grow there. In leveling a forest to provide for biomass energy, one will destroy or severely restrict the life habitats of these animals.

There are plenty of eco-groups which would be appalled by this sort of thing. On other words, boiling all of this down to its basics, we can say that biomass, apart from a few special cases, really isn't going to be anything of consequence.

Another version of the Biomass conceot would be geothermal energy which, as it name implies is a way of using what Americans might refer to as a "Hot Spring". The ground, principally as the result of a volcanic or "hot" area gives forth hot water; steam; or other allied products. This is energy and can be used as such and its proponents talk about this being an endless cycle of "free energy" because rainfall will replenish, within the earth, the hot water which is taken out.

This sounds fine but, again, it fails in practice. California looked at this, I am told, in the late 1980s and found that the rain water did not fall fast enough to replenish what was taken out for energy purposes. Given that California may be at the start of a 500 year drought, as some climatologists have claimed, this shortage of rainfall is not going to do the idea of geothermal energy much good at all! Forget it, again, except in areas where there might be a better balance between hot water and rainfall.

SEGMENT SIX

CHAPTER THREE

——— ✦ ✦ ✦ ✦ ✦ ✦ ———

OK, GERRY IS THERE ANYTHING YOU LIKE WHICH MAY ACTUALLY WORK? (WELL … YES, NOW THAT YOU MENTION IT!)

In this segment of the book (SEGMENT THREE), I have been discarding some of the more widely held ideas hand-over-fist. These are Wind Power, Solar Power, biomass, geothermal, and of course my favourite bête-noir, nuclear energy. So what is left? Well, there are two things which I personally like and which the politicians are apparently not that happy with.

These are not something which are well known outside of the ink-splashed ideas just mentioned, but it seems to be efficient for micro-scale generators. Therefore, is "micro" the way to go and not the huge and inefficient ideas which are routinely trumpted about? The above ideas are examples of this outworn "Bigger is better" concept.

One is the Bedini-Schoolgirl motor which I wish to write a little bit on and which has been derided as a "perpetual motion" machine by scientists. These words are merely a nasty way of simply saying that "this device can never work, stop wasting your time on it". Hmmm … sounds like the reception given to cold fusion, doesn't it?

The other possibility hasn't even been discussed at the Bedini level, but is sounds like something which is of the "common sense" variety. The theory is that mankind is killing itself by pumping huge amounts of carbon dioxide, carbon monoxide, and carbon anything-else-you-can-think-of, into the air. Gasoline engines have been excoriated by all of this, but why? The technology may well exist to take out of the atmosphere the stuff we put into it and to simply use it again! Presto! Atmosphere cleaned and energy demand met to a decent extent.

Sadly, I do not think we shall see either of these possibilities put into play. I have referred above to the derision which will be heaped on the Bedini-Schoolgirl motor. The "Schoolgirl" portion of this refers to a schoolgirl in the United States who had a science project to do for school (doesn't it always seem to be like this?) and was running late. Either, depending on whom you read, she got her inspiration from her father and his interest in magnets or saw something which triggered her mind to try something with magnets. She received a very high grade for her efforts (deservedly so!) and I have read that when her motor was started up, it was still running five days later! The trouble here is that this sort of thing did not get picked up by a major company and patented (which would effectively remove it from circulation as a serious consideration) because it is very simple to put together and use. The big thing here is that this device can be used on a micro-level instead of the usual macro-level which one usually associates with major breakthroughs. Make no mistake about it: is IS significant. It can be used, if there were a disaster affecting the economic dissemination of electric power, by individual homes quite easily. If one is of a conspiracy minded bent, one could say that the powers-that-be do not want this technology widely made known (sort of like cold fusion, it occurs to me) as there is no profit in it for captive corporations and that if there is a major outage of power for any reason (EMP attacks have been mooted once again in recent months) these controlling interests want people helpless and not "managing to get by" on a very small scale.

In any event, it is my considered opinion that if any of my readers want to investigate items which can be used, they could do a lot worse than the Bedini-Schoolgirl motor. I have seen this used in various formats on farms in Australia's remote outback with good success as well. The Falklands, if they were not so blessed with their abundant wind power, would find this device very useful as well.

And what can we say about the second of our two "unknown" technologies: that of reclaiming carbon from the atmosphere? This sounds rather obvious but it also lies in the area where the militant environmentalists have staked out their claims to fame. How often have you looked at news stories about the terrible damage to the Ozone layer (and every other layer it seems) which the endless burning of fossil fuels is doing? As far as I can see, it is the basis for the global warming theories (not yet proven I should add) and we are constantly told that we are all going to be fried, with our society and food supply destroyed. It is an effective marketing campaign to be sure and the last thing the opponents of this cleansing idea want to see (assuming its principals are looking to grab ultimate power from this – also written about, look it up!) is for the atmosphere to be scrubbed clean and thus allowing us to go back to the start of the industrial age and live life (with fancy cars no less!) as we see fit.

I would also imagine the major oil companies, blinded with the need for ever bigger bottom lines and dividends, would not be amused at a new and sudden burst of oil supplies being literally "mined from the skies". It is not going to go anywhere this "sky-cleansing" to give it a name; there is too much opposition. I just wanted you to be aware of yet another system of what might be an excellent form of pollution control.

SEGMENT SIX

CHAPTER FOUR

✦ ✦ ✦ ✦ ✦

HOW "GOD" TRADES OIL! MONEY FIRST, LAST, AND ALWAYS. WHY YOUR PUMP PRICES ARE HIGH...

Finally, I would like you to see how a major trader in the oil pits operates. He is nicknamed "God" and is rumored to work for either a major US bank or trading firm. See what you think!

One of the things which I find so appalling is how US brokerage firms trade (and encourage their client to do likewise). They seem to have no idea of what a trend is. One of the Rothschilds in Paris, about 150 years ago, said that the way to make money was to have an idea and let the market start to run with it (ie to see if your idea was correct). Then you buy in, with the trend most probably established, and observe what you were considering in the real world of financial markets. You watch it move and then when the market becomes really over-enthusiastic about the trend, you bail out. This is how you should trade and it should (if you are any good at what you are doing) net you large profits with little risk. In a move from say 100-300 in a stock (which we assume is your idea), you should let the gamblers take the first 40 points from 100 to 140 (or 20% of the entire proposed move). You step in and buy at 140 selling out at 260. The last 40 points you leave for all of the wild-eyed enthusiastic traders to overstay their welcome; ultimately to get crunched as the inevitable correction occurs. As I say, you can make serious money using this approach. You generally know you are correct by the way, if, when you sell, people are ridiculing you for selling "such an obvious money spinner" or some such. This is something I look for all the time!

What does the average American trader do (and this is why something like 17/20 lose money with most of the rest breaking even)? He may have an idea that something is going to happen in a certain stock and buys it. Fine and dandy with that, but then one of two things will happen. First, he will see a decent gain in the first week or so and immediately take profits on the idea that "profits do not take themselves". This person then misses most of the rest of the move waiting for "a pullback" to reenter the trade which never comes. The other possibility is that this person's idea is wrong and they will not admit it by selling out and taking a manageable loss, thereby ultimately losing most of their trading capital. Effectively they buy when their broker tells them to do so and likewise sell. They make next to nothing as just noted. They always think that losing money is "for someone else" and that "if I can just hang on I will be fine". In other words, I should never lose. PLEASE, find me a market which operates on this principle!

The real trader is "God" to get back on track here. As far as I can tell, he is an experienced floor trader trading crude oil futures. He has sold his senior management on the idea that "oil is going up" and is going to go up quite a long way. He is looking at the fundamentals, which his Board of Directors are probably considering as well. He looks at the market and sees endless backwardation which is getting larger (ie the shortages are getting worse). He then looks at what the major countries are doing as regards oil and sees that the informed money in those places is telling him that oil is something to go after as fast as possible. (Of course, you have to be able to read what this informed money is saying and doing!) For example, he sees Britain telling the Argentinian Government to back off from its dubious clams to the Falklands archipelago, and is actually building a 6000' airstrip on the very remote island colony of St. Helena in the South Atlantic Ocean. This facility can be used, if the Argentines needed any further prodding on this score, as a military base if it was deemed necessary. Of course we then see that the Falklands is sitting on what could be a motherlode of oil! He sees the possibility that the planners in the Kremlin have managed to bring The Crimea back into Russian hands, with possibly huge supplies of oil and Natural Gas offshore. We have all read about how China is looking to threaten Indonesia, Japan, Taiwan, Philippines, and now Viet Nam with border claims in the South China Sea where there is (surprise!) supposed to be vast oil deposits. This goes on and on with claims and counter claims and the like in Mali (France's "former" colony) and the Sudan/South Sudan in Africa, just to name two more places. There is even scuttlebutt about the US making eyes at Canada (see the earlier chapters on "The Merger") most probably because of the giant deposits in the Tar Sands.

In short, the fundamentals are bullish and informed money is trying to grab all it can get. This should mean that oil has, realistically, no nearby ceiling as to how far it can advance. "God" then makes his case to his Board of Directors who may be leaning the same way and they agree to back him all the way on this one. He therefore has acquired billions of dollars in credit he can fall back on to meet margin calls and the like, and he trades aggressively. He starts to be noticed (as he should be) in "the pits" and attracts gasps of awe at what he is doing. He acquires the somewhat blasphemous nickname of "God" because of his seemingly uncanny ability to turn markets in his direction and force less well capitalised traders to cover their positions from him at a premium. Being a long time trader myself, I can say that he trades in these tick-by-tick markets with a underlying idea of what oil should be doing at various levels because he understands these markets and what makes them go. His knowledge of the fundamentals is staggering and it shows. His Board of Directors can see him trade and what their returns are. They are, clearly, well pleased and needing all sorts of trading profits for their bottom line they let him continue. Using Rothschild's dictum noted above, I believe that it is very possible that while "God" trades in and out leaving less well capitalised traders (note: very important, you can't trade without capital) in the dust, he probably has a core position of contracts which he will not sell, and why should he? If he currently holds these at an average entry price of, say $ 85-90, he is well onside with a lot of padding in case something should go drastically wrong based on today's prices of $ 104 or so. He may well feel that oil will go to $ 150 or thereabouts, and this is his trading target. If he is correct about fracking's limited holding power, which I believe that he is, then on something like a holding of 10 million barrels he is going to make his principals a profit of roughly like $ 650 million, and that would be before any in and out trading profits are taken into consideration with technical adjustments on this core position. It is a nice chunk of money for the bottom line of a major financial institution which might be hurting these days!

What is the point of telling you how a corrupt system works anyhow? It is simply to inform you how the current shortage of oil is recognised by some bright people who are using it to make all sorts of money. The fact that you, the end consumer, are going to have to pay these profits (the $ 650 million comes from somewhere after all!) should tell you that oil and energy is in tight supply. It should also tell you that any pullbacks at the pump in prices are going to be short term and that you will see these price reductions reversed en route to ever higher charges at your future fill ups. "God" and others of his kind are doing nothing to increase the supplies available for society, but are making very sure that their pockets are going to be well lined for the ultimate day when governments around the world finally crack and have to tell their electorates that they are well and truly screwed. By this time, the big hitters are going to be nowhere to be found and are long since retired to a very nice existence! Thank you very much!

Well, now you know a little bit about the problems and possibilities (and the slippery politics, mustn't forget those now should we?!) which are in the energy segment of the global economy. I have NOT included any comments about coal (which the US has a huge reserve in places like Wyoming) as it is such an easy target for environmentalists who (literally) roll their eyeballs when people mention coal or coal gasification as a way around the growing shortages of the biggie – oil. Germans have a large quantity of brown coal in their country but the powerful environmental lobby there is most displeased at the prospects of large amounts of atmospheric contaminant being released when it is burned. However, given that the EU government in Brussels seems determined to allow fracking in Western Europe (for whatever that is worth given its limited shelf life), it would not surprise me to see brown coal burning being allowed in greater quantities there as well.

Have a good look at all of the bits and pieces I have put together here for you. Yes, you may disagree with some of them (Bedini-Schoolgirl?) but that is fine. All I want you to do is to analyse what the underlying problems are going forward (and there are many of them) and think about what all of this means to you and yours. Be aware and think! Now I must have a look at the underlying global politics in the last Segment of this book as this will also paint a picture (ugly, but a picture nevertheless!) of what is driving many nations these days. How are the powerful reacting? What happens to the weak and defenseless? Let's find out!

SEGMENT SIX

CHAPTER FIVE

$$\diamond \; \blacklozenge \blacklozenge \blacklozenge \blacklozenge \; \diamond$$

PENSIONS. WHAT A MESS! NO ROUND THE WORLD TRIPS FOR YOU IN YOUR GOLDEN YEARS, SORRY TO SAY.

Many years ago, when I was much younger, I can recall learned debates on this subject with many people saying that without at least ten workers to support one retiree, the system could not possibly work. Lots of press was devoted to this and because (in my opinion) it dealt with a problem many years down the road no one in Congress really cared. No tough decisions were made and we were just left to "muddle through". Even the retirement age was not raised, which I would have thought was quite obvious. Can't raise retitement ages now can we? It might lead to votes being lost for the Congressman who even proposed this sort of thing, much less voted for it! It was said that "Social Security was the third rail of politics: touch it and you die". So, with the backbone of marshmallows, Congress did the absolute minimum and look where we are now! All we have is that "Social Security will be there when you need it" and no math to back up what is probably this absurd claim: unless ... unless. Could it be that some far sighted people in Congress (Oh, come on! There are bound to be one or two in that lot!) have run some numbers and feel that with the arrival of scores of millions of immigrants that the FICA taxes will take care of the immediate problem? Maybe this is so, but what happens when this set of immigrants retire "some years down the road"? What happens to that crisis? Ah, fugitaboutit! That's then and not my problem. Once a marshmallow always a marshmallow! However, in the overall pension scheme, Social Security is just one piece of the puzzle. What else is there to worry about? Plenty!

What happens with corporate and State/Municipal pensions? What happens if you are about to be paid by Detroit or a Detroit wanna-be? What happens to private 401 – k plans (RRSP in Canada) which a person might have been contributing into all of their working lives? How will these fare if other plans are struggling to stay afloat? I read, when Detroit was sharing the spotlight of shame, that some public servants there who had worked for thirty years or so and were counting on a decent pension from the City were going to be sorely disappointed. One case saw someone who was counting on perhaps a $ 3000/month pension wound up looking at getting maybe 16 cents on the dollar – say $ 500/month if he was lucky. It seems that the finances in that wretched city are tangled and corrupt beyond measure.

Unions screaming for "more, more, ever more" and corruption on an apparent epic scale have decimated pension reserves until they are worth very little at all. Pensioners, in that luckless city, are to be paid in promises it seems. These were so eagerly believed in and life went on with promises as effective currency until it all came tumbling down, as it ultimately had to. Am I being unduly harsh on what was once "The Motor City"? No, there are others which are in a mess, but none on the scale of Detroit. However, what about the next step up: the individual States? There are two which I have been watching, and while they are not in the news at this time on this subject, the problems they face have not gone away. These are California (upon which the economic fate of the US probably depends, given its enormous size, economic depth and diversity) and Illinois. I do not think it is much of an exaggeration to say that the health of this latter state rests upon the "City of Broad Shoulders" which is, of course, Chicago. Unfortunately, as is with the case of nearby Michigan, too much of this state rests on the health of one city (Michigan rising or falling, mostly falling, with Detroit) – and this is Chicago.

The unions and a series of city administrations have done the pension system there no good at all and some of the pension funds there are about 40-50% funded only. What does this mean? It means that out of every dollar in pension payment liabilities, the paying authority has between 40 and 50 cents in assets. Normally when a pension falls to as low as 80 cents on the dollar it is time for remedial action, so you only guess how pension managers there must be tearing their hair out these days! In my experience, a well run pension fund has 100 cents on the dollar (or more) to match liabilities. In reading up on all of this, I am astounded that Chicago seems to have no real concerns at its appalling level of funding, and I wait for the day when the headlines blare that "Chicago pensioners will have to take a 'haircut' (discount) because of the poor state of the books". I can't see how this can be avoided to be frank and I pity the poor pensioners who will wake up one morning to a letter which starts "Dear Sir/Madam, we regret to inform you that due to problems beyond our control, we are cutting the amount of your monthly pension check to $ 1500 from $ 3000". It is coming; bet on it. A case of corruption run amok, I would say.

California (I hadn't forgotten them either) has done unbelievably stupid things with its pension liabilities and as is the case with so many other entities around the US seems to have regarded the pot of money put aside as some sort of slush fund to be used when it is politically necessary. Pensions need a lot of time to grow their assets to make their payments. They also require an annual average return of about 8% to make these payments work mathematically at the end (ie what you get in your final payment when you turn 60 or 65 or whenever). What many people do not realise is that it is the compounding effect of all of these returns which really juice up the payouts. By the way, while I think about it, you may have read about funding many decimated pension plans (and this may ultimately include Social Security) by hiking the monthly premiums on your paycheque. This means, in plain English, your deductions are going to go quite a bit higher. We should also note that this concept of compounding is going to make itself felt here as well.

If you are only a few years from retirement, then maybe you will not be hit on your pay as much as someone who is twenty-five let us say. Why is this? If you are twenty-five, then your contributions have a full forty years to compound. If you are sixty, then the compounding factor is effectively irrelevant. Your pension fund will go (as everybody else does!) where the money is – and, needless to say, how it is generated. For example, if we look at a return of 8% per annum (simple interest) on your contribution of $ 100 after thirty years, we would see it worth $ 340. If we compound this 8% at 8% (that is to say your return of 8% is in turn reinvested at 8% for each and every year you contribute) we get something quite different. Then your $ 100 would be worth $ 1000 (ten times as much versus just $ 340 in a simple interest calculation) and that makes the entire system work. If we remove some of the compounding for whatever reason (ie corruption or whatever) then the returns take quite a hit. To boil this paragraph down, I have seen some cities in California showing a return of just 1.5%. This is bad, BAD news if you are retiring a few years from now.

Am I intending to frighten you? Yes, quite frankly, I am! No, I do not take some sort of sadistic pleasure in doing this, but it is mandatory in the remaining years before the pension math collides with reality that I tell all and sundry about my fears. No matter what you hear from embarrassed and embattled pension boards, just keep in mind that large amounts of cash are require to pay pensioners (Baby-Boomers) month in and month out. Keep in mind also that increased payouts will be required as inflation protection riders kick in; and kick in without limit as time goes by. So what, you may say? You would claim that this is allowed for in the calculations when the pensions were set up, and you would be right (up to a point). However if more and more cash has to be paid out, then either more cash has to be taken in from pension dues when the Baby-Boomers were working (and now their successors), or there has to be a better return for the fund.

Now if pension funds have an interruption in their flow on money for some years (as has happened under the very easy money policy by the Fed for a lengthy period of time now), where is this extra money going to come from especially if pensions exist on the magic of compound interest? With inflation riders, the squeeze on returns even at 8% is probably close to absolute and any breakdown in these forms of income will simply not be available to be made up. What about individual pension plans – the so-called 401 – k plans? Aren't these going to save the day; those people who could afford to put money aside to fund them in an age of squeezed paychecks and the like? I do not believe so. In assessing a study of how people manage money on the Chicago Board of Trade, we see some truly dismal numbers. Some years back it was claimed that out of every twenty traders, fully nineteen of them (that is 95%) lose money. A more recent study shows that traders are doing a bit better with "just" 17/20 losing money – or 85%. This means that nearly all people who trade to try and boost the derisory returns available from the interest rate markets are simply not making it shall we say. When one adds in the fees taken by the trustees who hold the monies or invest on behalf on individuals, the overall success rate is quite dismal. Clearly, and this is another way of putting it, if society was expecting people to be able to provide for themselves in their old age, it is not going to be the case.

So, to avoid all of the problems associated with a lack of pension income for the elderly starting literally anytime going forward, something will have to be done. However, it seems to this observer, that while there were as many trillions as needed to bailout the US banking system after its absurd attempt to make dud mortgages sound (the terrible mortgage crisis starting in late 2007 which nearly toppled every other banking system across the globe), none will be made available to assist pensions. It would be held (and this would definitely be true if a right-wing Republican wins the White House in 2016) that this "something" would be "socialist intervention" in a free market economy which is something the average American does not stand for. OK, so maybe I am being a little harsh here with my criticism, but there is an underlying point to all of this: where is the money coming from to do all of the bailing? We hear today deafening cries that President Obama is bankrupting America for generations to come with his free spending ways and these know-it-all critics point to the staggering (at present writing) accumulated federal deficit of $ 17.5 trillion. This is very unfair because, without Congressional consent, the US president cannot spend a dime of taxpayer money. However it is the perception which matters. No matter who wins in 2016 (and I am of the firm belief that it will be Mrs. Clinton) the cries about "the pension deficit" will be unending. Yes, I know what I have written about the likely GOP response to this mess, but something will have to be done whether the GOP likes it or not. The difference will be one of degree. Where is a large enough clump of money, anywhere, to accomplish all of this pension reform anyway? Some of the right-wing blogs have been floating a trial balloon that all (note this word) pensions will have to be nationalised and most likely merged with Social Security.

You would then get one monthly cheque from the SS Administration instead of one from them, one from your former employer or employers, and whatever you can scrounge from your own 401 – k. This will be very bad news for the few who have been able, one way or another, to provide for themselves and their families and perhaps these few should have a long think as to what to do with their (so-far) profitable portfolios. Perhaps cashing out a sizeable portion of it and buying gold?? I am, of course, guessing and I would imagine that older and wiser heads than mine have considered this and many other possibilities. Many years ago, I read that perhaps 2/3 of retired Americans (back then) only had their monthly SS cheque as their sole income. They lived in desperate poverty and were, literally, one illness away from being completely bankrupted. What a harrowing way to live! Of the remaining 33% of retired Americans, perhaps 25% were just getting by with a small degree of comfort with SS cheques and whatever else they were lucky enough to be able to acquire during their working lives. Only the remaining 10% (or less) were able to live their retirements as they may have imagined throughout their lives. This was quite pathetic, at the time I read this, and I wondered just how these poor souls had been so badly misled with their pension funds. Surely, something would be done? Well, a few years ago I re-visited the problem and found to my amazement that 2/3 of Americans still had SS only to tide them over. There were a couple of percentage points different in the other two categories, but that was it! Why do I point this out? I merely want to say that the endless barrage of "buy that new car or new house; you owe it to yourself" which the average free spending American is subject to through his/her working life, has been responsible for what we are witnessing today.

The "good life" has conquered all rational views of how life should be lived and it therefore stands to reason that the response to the now unstoppable pension crisis (and that word is not misused sorry to say) will be handled in a similar fashion: don't worry, good times will still roll. This is, of course, quite impossible looking at the numbers, so what IS to be done? As the title of this book asks: "What ... IS ... happening"? Don't worry your sweet little heads about it! Uncle Sam will take care of it as he has taken care of just about everything so far. The bottom line will be that SS will bail out everybody and everything, to an extent, and that everybody will have – as the end result – some sort of living monthly stipend. There will be all sorts of conditions laid out, all of which will be said to "ensure the solvency of Social Security virtually indefinitely". The age of eligibility for SS will be raised, possibly at one step, from 62 to 66 and then to 70 to cut down on the number of early retirees which the math underlying SS simply cannot support. There will be (because of the vast number of Americans who have nothing but SS when they retire) a conversion of SS to some sort of "means tested" programme, which, in simple terms, says that if you are making over $ 50,000 when you retiree then you do not "need" the basic SS payment; you will have to get by on your own resources and inputed company pension plans (this is the part which has been absorbed into SS as noted above), but not the SS basic payment. It will not be pretty, unless you are very poor and are now feeling better that so many others have been dragged down to your level. The other possibility is something which I am seeing in South Korea. There is more to this Asian powerhouse than opposition to North Korea and the making of Hyundai motor cars. A series of articles in the newspaper Chosen Ilbo for June 9, 2014 talks about the plight of Koreans under their version of Social Security. Because it is a weak system (how else do you think that the funding of the Korean economic miracle after the devastating war from 1950-53 was obtained?) these Koreans will probably have to work until they are 71 years old or so. Forty percent of the retiring Baby Boomers are going to be living in penury in retirement. Fifty percent need a stipend from their children to make ends meet, which makes one wonder how these children are going to be able to fund having families of their own and hence overcome the Fertility Rate problem for their country which we discussed previously. (Knee bone connected to the thigh bone). Finally, many Koreans associate retirement with loneliness and poverty in any event. It is a ghastly scenario and one which, I am afraid to say, awaits so many elderly Americans who were told that "the system will make you secure in your retirement" and that "Social Security will be there when you need it". Well I suppose that it is to some extent, but it seems a fair bet that it is not what many Americans had envisioned for themselves in their Golden Years. Let's finish off this segment of the book by pasting what I had to write about retirement in the newsletter. Yes, there will be some duplication of material from what has gone before, but I want you to see how it all continues to fall together:-

"There has been a fair bit of commentary recently on this subject in the blogs and also 'regular' channels. Being an elderly gentleman myself (!), and a fully fledged pensioner, it behooves me to at least have a look at all of this. I have had several letters from some readers (thank you, DK – and others) who do not wish to accept all of the bad news which I so routinely pour out in these newsletters. "Well, I am sorry with all of this apparent negativity, but I have to call things in the way that forty-six years of training has taught me! The overall situation is unremittingly grim as we look forward immediately into 2014, and then into the problems of the 2015-2020 period. Debt is the main killer here on many fronts, from overstretched consumers who simply cannot say a simple 'No' to the latest bit of hi-tech glitter, to governments who are generally over indebted; badly so in many cases.

"Whether it is a consumer who simply says 'I gotta have this gizmo – it is sooo me', or a government which never met a war or security issue it didn't like, debt is debt and it is an immense killer of citizens and nations. "Why do I bring this up when it comes to the subject of pensions and the like? Well, pension funds have to invest large amounts of money for their clients and the huge debt issues running roughshod through the global economies are causing all sorts of grave distortions. "For example in the early part of this century, home loans (mortgages) have been forced to become more borrower-friendly so as to keep what was an over priced housing market from falling apart. The net result of all of this was the fiasco in 2007/2008 which nearly resulted in a complete collapse of banking systems everywhere. As of today it is my understanding that banks are still in a dreadful to-do on their balance sheets from this mortgage mess and are speculating in various financial markets in what may termed close to insanity as regards positioning. "I, of course, refer you back to 'God'(earlier in the book) and his immense oil positions noted for some time now. Into these various messes comes the poor pension manager. With long term interest rates now at only something slightly shy of 4%, other things have to be tried.

"Why is this? I was shown some interesting figures recently which clearly demonstrated just how stressed pension funds really are. We are looking at a minimum of an 8% return on assets to be able to meet the future demands of pensioners. Now it is clear that 4% Treasury returns (at best) will not be able to cover an 8%+ call on assets. What I had failed to consider adequately was the compounding effects of liabilities versus these assets. "The study I saw used a figure of 9% for liabilities and I suppose that is reasonable, but what I failed to look at properly (!) was the compounding effect of all of this. Simply put, if assets are to cover liabilities then the assets must grow at the same rate as pension liabilities. The trouble with all of this (as any pension manager will tell you) is that whatever happens, the liabilities are going to grow and grow. This negative growth (overall pension fund health essentially) will be there whatever happens to the asset side of your pension's balance sheet. "If we have a problem with interest rate receipts from a failing bond market (this is, of course, in terms of interest payable to the pension fund) then a gap will quickly emerge and will, unless checked, simply get larger and larger (ah, the magic of compound growth on the wrong side of the ledger!). "So, what is a fund manager to do? What is s/he allowed to do under law? Does a certain amount of the pension's assets have to be invested in US Treasuries? Can so-called 'speculative trades' be allowed? The king of all of these bond pensions is the mainstay of the US system and that is Social Security. This has to be invested in US Treasury bonds and so, these days, SS is suffering with interest rate yields on its portfolio probably not keeping pace with the burgeoning baby boom retirees. "Yes, this sort of demographic bulge can be allowed for in initial calculations, but if anything goes wrong with (let us say) Congress raiding what must be a very tempting financial pot, then how is it to be made up? It is a long way from my parents paying in something like $ 3 a month to fund their retirement, to the maximum annual contribution of $ 7,049.40 today. Is this sort of mark-up reflecting what has been added to and re-assigned by Congress to the SS system over the decades? "What else can be given to SS to fund as the overall economic situation (as measured by the yearly deficit) forces Congress to look for large quantities of money which have not yet been assessed for tax revenue purposes? The main problem here for SS, given its exposure to bonds, must be if the new Fed Chairman, Janet Yellen, allows interest rates to drift down to a negative level. "What happens to a bond portfolio if, instead of receiving interest from the federal government, it has to pay for the privilege of holding US financial paper? (In other words, interest rates become negative). If SS has to pay out to retirees and also to the federal treasury, then it will soon have to dip into its overall assets/reserves to continue to make all of the required payments. Again, with this sort of major upset of baby boom retirement payments, we are going to see significant problems come forward for Congress to address once again. "It will not be pleasant to watch (or to fund, come to think of it) what is done to rectify these problems and my personal belief is that the conservatives in those august bodies may simply allow SS to rollover and die in what they believe is a long overdue death. "There appear to be many such legislators who simply do not believe that SS was ever meant to be, or is at best, some giant and unaffordable Ponzi Scheme. In reality it is what so many other pension funds are: a way for the elderly to live with a modicum of dignity in their declining years. "If it is not to be abolished in some manner, then (and this is my favourite given the incredible money problems which the US currently suffers from) it will be sold off/privatised with all that this may imply for grandpa and grandma's monthly benefit cheques. (Hint: in this case think of great volatility in monthly payouts as the acquiring banks will want to grind the funds they are acquiring to generate some good trading profits. Granny and gramps will probably not participate, benefit-wise, in this trading orgy to any great extent).

"I have heard from some of my readers that it is impossible to sell off SS to banks or to anybody else. Why, these people ask, would anybody want to buy up a bankrupt fund which is composed of government bonds which are on the verge of suffering a great calamity within a few years now? The clear implication is that such paper (full faith and credit) is effectively worthless and who on earth would buy paper which is either valued impaired now or will be in just a few short years? "With all liabilities and no assets, SS will be exposed for what so many conservative Congressmen believe: a worthless Ponzi scheme. I disagree, provided that the sale of SS takes place when the value of US Treasuries is still unquestioned by the markets as a whole. This would have to be fairly soon, if it is going to happen at all. "If the Fed will act as a buyer of last resort for this paper, then cash can still be obtained from such a sale. Let us see how all of this plays out. SS is in a mess to be sure, but if the US$ on global exchange markets holds up then perhaps more time can be gained. Don't get ahead of yourself in other words!

"I mention SS in some depth as it is probably the bluest of the blue chip funds. What about others, which would include other state and local pensions and so on down to corporate and then individual funds? The article which I have been referring to (by Ben Inker of the firm Bridgewater, I believe) has assessed this in depth. "The big thing which stuck me so forcefully, is what this compounding can really do. There is an excellent chart in the analysis which I am not able to reproduce here which shows that by next year (ie not some far off date which means little to most people) US public pension funds will be showing an asset/liability gap of something like $ 1.2 trillion. How is this to be made up? Can it be funded at all? The asset/liability mismatch was well managed until the mortgage debacle in 2007/08 when desperately needed capital gains from equities simply were not there because equities completely fell apart. Mortgage debacles will do that to a pension fund! "In assessing all of the foregoing, before I wrote this piece (and saw Inker's exceptional analysis), I believed that the current great run up in stocks would have covered whatever temporary shortfall may have occurred back then. This seems not to be the case. Allowing for this damnable liability compounding and, very probably, some drawdown of the asset base to pay "temporary benefits" to retirees, market losses (more accurately "lack of gains") have not yet been redeemed from current price improvements. "This is another way of writing what I have been saying in the last few sentences. In turn, this can only imply, with the derisory returns from bonds, that public pension funds are in a dreadful mess. To underline this, we can only recall that the City of Detroit seems to have been rather creative with its accounting assumptions for its public pensions (from what I have read in some area newspapers) and now, with various claims against the fund and the city, it may be able to pay out only sixteen cents ($ 0.16) on the dollar to needy pensioners. "These poor folk seem to have been betrayed/sacrificed on the altars of political expediency during their working lives. The promise that "It will be there when you need it" has proven to be so similar to other such promises: hollow when monetary push comes to payment shove. "Well, all of this sounds like rather high and grandiose verbiage, so where is the one thing I always look for, which is Follow the Money? Yes, it is here as well. We need look no further than Mr. Ben Bernanke and the Federal Reserve.

"For sometime now, this once symbol of financial probity has been ladling out the sum of $ 85 billion a month to its member banks, by buying US Treasuries (and some mortgages) and printing the money to pay for them. The banks have been the big beneficiaries here as their ruined balance sheets from the 2007/08 mortgage mess remain in grave condition. These institutions, from what I can determine, have been using this money to make money by speculating to a fare-the-well in just about anything that trades. "Any and all derivatives are fair game here and I wonder what the average citizen would think if s/he knew that with this printed money the banks would be trading in such instruments as option spreads on interest rate barbells? (Don't ask!) "However, it is the stock market which interests me here. All day and every day I seem to be reading all about 'How the Dow is grossly overpriced by all objective measures' and why it is due for a crash of historic proportions. However, this is not the case to date. If one follows the flow of funds, one sees that equities are strongly bullish and likely to remain that way. Money is pouring into equity funds of all descriptions and the Dow is strongly bid, to put it mildly! The target here is Dow 19,000. "Yes, I am aware that in 2014 we shall probably have a medium sized war somewhere or other and wars are not good for equities. However, this would be the correction which so many people are awaiting in my view. If we then have a moderately quick conflict and then the bond crisis in 2015, equities may move sharply higher – all to the benefit of badly damaged pension funds. "It is the belief of many analysts that Mr. Bernanke's largesse in buying bonds (QE or $ 85 billion a month) was really designed to increase the value of equities to try and bail out desperately flailing pension funds. I would agree with this, although because of the misery of stock losses in 2007/08 and the inexorable grinding of compound liabilities, I do not think it will be even close to being enough assistance and will only gain a bit of time until something more dramatic will have to be seen. "However as we have been wondering in previous newsletters, it is more likely that the Fed leader Janet Yellen, is going to wind up doing the reverse. Oh, granted that she will try to crank up the economy with more of the Bernanke ultra-easy money policy, but that is having a terrible effect on bond holders. Interest rates yielding less than 4% are useless for long term capital appreciation, as we have been discussing. "The real problem for pension funds must therefore be what happens if she lets interest rates fall to negative levels (see above). People will be seeing the value of their bank accounts fall, possibly dramatically depending on just how far Yellen lets rates fall. "Equities, in this environment, will do well. Think about this. If you have a choice between paying a bank 1-2% a year to watch your chequing account, or investing in a name company which pays a dividend of +3% what are you going to do?

"It is fairly obvious I would have thought, especially if you are a long term holder such as a pension fund. True, it is not enough to offset the accrued liabilities which are compounding (back to that again), and this will still probably ultimately sink pension funds – purely on a cash flow basis. "However, if the Dow runs to 31,000 (as I saw in an ultra-bullish ad today) then maybe you are still all right. However, if you need the Dow to run to 31,000 (possibly higher with some Dow components) then you are really having to back to the edge of a cliff to do your fighting. It is all so very dangerous, no matter what the US authorities try. "The damage to the real economy done by ultra-low interest rates to date (and heading lower if my prognosis is correct) has been to twist it and stretch it in unnatural ways, to the detriment of all. "One thing I should mention here is what may happen if pension funds start to go down in large numbers with several million old age citizens not being able to collect enough to live on and, consequently, being reduced to penury. My sense is that something will have to be done about this, given what may be a very real fear by the Central Authorities of mounting disquiet in the citizenry as things go from bad to worse. "We have had a look-see at what SS and (in all probability) State and local pension funds are going to be going through. The money will not be there in anything like what has been promised, as the accruals simply do not make the sense required to do this. So, when many other US cities (and States like Illinois and possibly California) start to use what will probably be called 'The Detroit Formula' by going through bankruptcy as a means of getting their books in order, what will be done? "One cannot have possibly scores of towns and cities simply deciding that pensioners will get it in the neck at sixteen cents on the dollar because the banks or other preferred creditors are demanding (and receiving through a compliant court system) their pound of flesh.

"The outcry will be deafening and even hard core GOP Members of Congress, who may entertain severe doubts about the whole idea of public pensions (ie SS, as noted above), will not be able to resist "doing something". What will probably happen is that the bankrupt pension funds (or nearly so) will probably be folded into SS in some manner. "This would be doubly attractive if the banks are in the process of taking over SS. As this would represent a possibly serious cost to the taxpayer, we shall be told that 'those responsible will be brought to justice' and the American version of very public show trials will be witnessed by all and sundry. Justice must at least be seen to work! "As regards corporate pension plans, I have had two instances of first hand experience as to how corporations will use just about any trick to try and bring back, onto the corporate balance sheet, what are deemed 'excess returns' which the pension manager happens to make in a given year. "I would have considered that this was a very good way to see corporate pension funds to be something less than what may have been promised (either explicitly or implied) to a soon-to-be pensioner. If there are a lot of pensioners in this position, what are we to make of corporate pension funds? Will they be treated in a similar fashion to failing state pensions? My guess is that they will be, simply because who is going to differentiate between poor pensioners under the state or company system?

"Lastly, what about private pensions: the legendary 401 - k which has been around for so long? Here it may be a little bit different. There may be quite a few plans which have done what they were supposed to. They, the plan holders, will have worked diligently to provide for themselves and their families. Yes, there will be some plan holders who will have had no idea what they were doing for the last few decades and the plan they were contributing to has proven to be a bust. There will be those who have invested (because they REALLY know what they were doing) in Nikkei Put spreads and exotica such as this, and have done well. These professionals will be few and far between however. What will happen here? "Will ALL private plans be agglomerated with SS with all sorts of other plans so that the plan holders will now be 'fully protected' against what might happen when the plan is drawn down to pay for retirement needs? I don't know (fairly obviously) but I would guess that only those who have lost money or who do not have enough assets for their pension will be rescued. "However, it is quite possible that with out of control federal spending that the 'winners' here might be obliged to purchase US federal bonds as some sort of act of solidarity. If there is the bond crisis occurring at that time (as I have written about in the past) this might be akin to a form of confiscation of financial assets. If the overall situation is as bad as all of this implies, then we may see something along these lines. A desperate Washington will go after the money where they can find it!

"To sum all of this up succinctly, let me say that I am sorry. Apart from a few company pension plans and a precious few individuals who really know what they are doing, the vast majority of Americans (and people elsewhere, as what happens in the US tends to be reflected across the globe) are going to have a series of unpleasant surprises come the age of 65 (probably 70 or higher in reality, although governments seem to be so slow in recognising the age factor here). A mess to be sure, and I do not see how the rules of math can be realigned to "make it all go away". That ship has unfortunately sailed." (End of lengthy newsletter quotes)

Well, that's it for all of my ponderings on "What ... IS ... Happening". I just wanted all of my readers to have an idea about everything I have been writing about (and I could have gone on for MUCH longer with so many other problems in the world) and how all of this WILL affect them. It is just a question of when. Now let's sum it up in a brief epilog and then let you think – for yourselves please, and not what the press is telling you and has been telling you for your entire life. That ship has also sailed, and it is time for you to THINK FOR YOURSELVES!

www.ingramcontent.com/pod-product-compliance
Lightning Source LLC
Chambersburg PA
CBHW071257190726
48292CB00007B/2571